Murder is Handy

Sharon McGregor

Whimsical Publications, LLC

Florida

Murder is Handy is a work of fiction. Names, characters, and incidents are the products of the author's imagination and are either fictitious or are used fictitiously. Any resemblance to actual events or persons, living or dead, is entirely coincidental.

To purchase the authorized electronic edition of *Murder is Handy*, visit www.whimsicalpublications.com

Cover art by Janet Durbin
Editing by Brieanna Robertson

ISBN-13: 978-1-63495-034-3

Published by
Whimsical Publications, LLC
Florida

"I told you Jonah was not a nice person. I found out personally a couple of years ago when he did some work for me."

"Didn't finish the job or do the work properly?"

"Nothing like that. Actually he was very good at what he did. No, it was after the work was done and I was about to pay him the amount he quoted. Suddenly he upped the amount. I told him that wasn't the agreed price and he began to talk about my relationship with your Aunt Grace."

"He didn't!"

"Grace came over here often and I guess while he was working here he must have put two and two together and worked out what our relationship was."

"But you would never give in to blackmail!"

"Of course not. Jonah thought in a small town, I might not want people to know our relationship. I told him he could tell whomever he wanted, that the town already knew and didn't care."

"How did he react to that?"

"He backed down pretty quickly, said that's not what he meant at all and went back to the original quote."

"So," said Taylor slowly. "If he tried it on with you, there may be others in town he tried it on. And other people might have cared more than you about their personal lives being known."

"I should have paid more attention to him after that. But how could I warn people? I couldn't very well take out an ad in the paper and say Jonah tried to blackmail me. Hide your secrets."

"If you tell Andrew, I imagine it will give him a line to follow. Other than that, who would want to kill him? He always seemed a friendly fellow and yet..."

"And yet what?"

"Did you notice at the coffee shop, it was so different from last year when Jennie and Tara Lynn died. Everyone was shocked then and maybe gossiped a lot, but they were genuinely sorry. You could see it in their faces."

Edie finished her thought. "But with Jonah, it was no more than conversation about something that happened in town, there was no grief in anyone's voices."

"Sad, isn't it? I wonder if Andrew will track down the sister. Or if she'll even care either."

"She might. It was the father she ran away from, not Jonah."

"But what about Brenda's comment about the men happy to see the back of him? Sounds like there must be at least one or two women in town who might mourn him. If it's true, that is."

Edie frowned a little and said. "If he did have a romantic interest, it was probably with a married woman," she said. "I've never seen him around town in the company of a anyone, so he's been pretty discreet about his relationships. Of course I'm not out on the town, but I'm sure I'd know if he was seeing someone in the open."

"I wonder how Brenda knows."

"Minister's wife?'

"Yes, her husband gave her a look after she made that comment. She probably knows a lot about people she can't divulge. So does he, of course."

"I know before Jonah went away, he left a trail of affairs behind him. Of course none of that would matter now. And he wasn't so circumspect then, so everyone knew who he was going with."

Taylor wasn't so sure it wouldn't matter. She knew from experience old history could spring up when least expected.

She went back to her cinnamon bun, but not with as much enjoyment as when she started. She tried to picture Jonah riding along in his pickup, dog riding shotgun, and couldn't reconcile that with the person she now knew he was.

"There's one person who will miss him," Taylor said. "Monty."

Chapter One

Jonah Whitcomb whistled through his teeth as he bumped the blue pickup along the byways of the nuisance grounds. He wasn't whistling a recognizable tune, just expressing his pleasure at the way the day had gone. There were others, he knew, that wouldn't look at things in the same way.

The garbage dump, known to residents as the "nuisance grounds" occupied what used to be a gravel pit. It had expanded and slid like a glacier over the years. As well as the depository for the garbage from the town trash collectors, there were areas for old building supplies, and a shed for electronics as well as bins for recycling.

The black and white dog beside Jonah appeared to be smiling too. He struggled to keep his balance on the truck seat beside his owner, but his joy at the happiness of his master was obvious. It was late afternoon and no one was in the grounds except for Jonah and his companion. The man paid by the town to supervise the garbage would be gone home for his supper. A gate stood across the main entrance but Jonah slid it open and then closed behind him. He didn't need help. He was a regular and knew where to go.

Jonah pulled to a halt at the north end of the grounds and backed his truck against an incline. This was the area used to dump old building materials and occupied the furthest reaches of the dump. Beyond lay a stand of trees and past that, the town cemetery.

He made short work of empting the truck box of the old

planks, two by fours and other debris from the project he had completed. He smacked his hands against his jeans to dislodge bits of sawdust that had clung to his clothes and spoke to his travelling companion through the truck window. "Good job, today, old fellow." The dog responded with a thwack of his tail against the back of the seat. His panting tongue disappeared for a moment in a gulp, then reappeared, hanging at the side of his mouth.

Jonah walked around the front of the truck to the driver's side and stood with his right foot on the running board, his back to the trees. Pulling a pack of cigarettes from his jacket pocket, he tapped the box and pulled one out, placing it between his lips. He cupped his hands, struck a match, and held it to the cigarette.

He smoked in silence for a bit, chuckling softly once in a while at the day's events. He flicked the cigarette stub to the ground and was grinding it into the dirt when he felt an unexplainable uneasiness. He started to jerk his head around at the sudden warning bark from the dog in the truck, but it was too late. A hard blow to the head felled him and another two followed. After that, Jonah felt nothing. The figure that had wielded the blow disappeared as fast as it had come.

The dog barked, clawing at the window to escape but there was no give to it and he couldn't expand the mere inch or two it was open. Bouncing back and forth from one side of the truck to the other, his howls began to mingle with the barks. He lunged at the driver's door, then crouched in the seat, scratching at the door. Finally, one of his paws hit the door handle with enough force and in the right direction to swing the driver's door open.

He leaned over Jonah, pawing at his shoulder as though to wake him, whimpering as he nuzzled his face, frightened by the lack of response and by the blood oozing from his head. He dropped into a crouch, stretching his body alongside Jonah's and became still.

Then, as though coming to a decision, he rose and began to lope off to the entrance of the grounds. He followed the winding road to the edge of town. He turned into a street and came to a stop in front of the first building on the corner. He trotted up to the door and sat on the ground, raising his head to begin a keening howl.

Chapter Two

Taylor Armstrong was sitting in front of her computer, her forehead lined with concentration and a little frustration. Her latest project wasn't going as she had hoped. She thought it was time to give it a rest for the day and hope for better results tomorrow, but she hated to end a day's work on a negative note.

A grey tabby cat sat on the corner of her desk. He stretched slightly, yawned and moved closer to the computer, patting at the closest keys.

"You think it's time to call it a day too," said Taylor. "You're probably right, I'm not getting anywhere and you're going to start putting in your two cents worth, aren't you?" Denver liked to position himself close to the computer and loved to play with the keys. Taylor wasn't sure if it was the heat from the device that attracted him, or if he looked on the computer as a rival for her attentions. Whatever it was, once he decided to join the action, she knew it was a lost cause.

The door to the bedroom she had converted into her office swung open and a Jack Russell appeared, head cocked to one side. "Okay, I'm done for the day. I know when I'm outnumbered. It's time for a walk for you, Tristan, and Denver, you leave the computer alone till I get back. Then we'll all have some supper."

To be on the safe side, she clicked the button to shut down the computer. You never could tell what a cat did when you weren't looking. She didn't trust Denver with access to her e-mail.

She went in search of Tristan's leash, but when she went to attach it to his collar, they both froze. A haunting keening howl was coming from outside, not far away. Tristan whimpered and barked at the noise, then looked at Taylor expectantly as though she should be fixing the problem.

"You stay here," Taylor said to Tristan and opened the front door a crack. She soon realized the howling was coming from next door, at Edie's Boarding Kennel. She pushed Tristan back from the door and shut it firmly in his face.

She approached the driveway next door slowly, peering around the hedge, wondering what could cause a dog to howl in that way. She wished she'd grabbed her phone. If it were an injured animal, she'd call Vivian, the vet.

Sitting in front of the Kennel door was a black and white Border collie, his head thrown back, howling at the entry. She approached him cautiously, thinking the dog looked familiar, but she couldn't place him. He turned to face her and began to whimper. He had a patch of what looked to be blood on his muzzle but didn't seem to be injured.

Certain that he had her attention, he began to leave the driveway, looking back as though inviting her to follow. He reminded her of the old Lassie shows, where the dog went for help. She was pretty sure that's just what this one was doing, but why was he here? She wasn't going anywhere without her phone, so she went back inside to retrieve it. The dog began to howl again, so she quickly ran outside and began to follow him.

Why was he at the kennel? Could he be one on the dogs Edie was boarding? She wanted to call and ask her but the collie wasn't giving her time to stop, He was very insistent. He led her down the road to the town nuisance grounds, and picked up speed as he went. Taylor was trying not to stumble along the uneven ground.

She hoped the dog wasn't taking her to an injured animal, maybe a dangerous one if it were hurt and frightened.

She could see a truck at the side of the grounds, parked, but with the driver's door hanging open. Beside the door was a pile of something, maybe clothes, or garbage. The dog ran straight ahead to the truck and she soon realized the pile of clothes was a person, a man, and he wasn't moving.

The dog looked from the man to her and back again, as though pleading with her.

Taylor knelt down beside him and saw the blood pooled beside his head. She leaned forward and touched her finger to his neck, searching for a pulse. She couldn't find one but wasn't sure if she were even feeling in the right place.

Thank heavens she'd stopped to bring her phone. She called emergency for an ambulance.

The dog lay down beside his master again. Now Taylor recognized both him and the man. It was Jonah, the local odd job man. The collie dog was always with him riding shotgun in the truck. The open truck door had hidden the writing that announced to the world *The Handyman Can*.

Chapter Three

The nuisance grounds was soon a hive of activity. Police cars and an ambulance surrounded the blue truck. Taylor stood to the side, shivering a little. Part of the shivering was from the cool of the approaching evening but part of it was fear. It was obvious to her that Jonah hadn't fallen and hurt himself which meant someone else was responsible.

It wasn't the type of thing you expected in a small town, although Taylor knew from experience dark shadows knew no boundaries. The town of Badger Lake was just getting over the tragedies from last summer. She hoped a new round of trouble wasn't about to start.

She was just going to ask Andrew if she could go home now when the RCMP sergeant approached her. Andrew Scott was six foot three with the build of a cowboy, lean but muscular. His police jacket gave him an added bulk that made him look imposing, even to Taylor who knew the softer side of him.

"How did you manage to find him?" he asked. "I didn't think the garbage dump was on your dog-walking route," He looked around. "And where is Tristan?"

Taylor explained about the dog and how he had led her here. "Is it all right if I leave now?"

"Sure," said Andrew, "I'll come over and talk to you later. It will take the forensic team time to get to town, so it may be a while."

She turned to leave, happy to be going away from the

smell and feel of death. Andrew called after her, "Do you think you could take the dog to Edie?" he asked. "He's getting in the way here."

"I don't know if he'll come with me," she said. "He's not going to want to leave Jonah."

"I think he knows now Jonah is dead. He's gone from anxious to resigned. I'll see if I can get a rope for a leash. We'll give it a try if that's all right with you."

"Okay." She might as well be of some use. She pulled out her phone and called Edie. "I have a new boarder for you," she said. "I can't talk now. I'll explain when we get there."

Andrew brought the dog over with a yellow cord attached to his collar as a leash. The dog sat down, head low, a picture of grief, but he seemed to cooperate.

"Oh, one thing," said Andrew. "Tell Edie to put him in a separate kennel and not to wash him or touch him any more than she has to. That goes for you too. I'm sure forensics will want to examine him. I don't know what good it will do since he's been contaminated already, but we'll try to keep him as clean as we can."

Bristling a little at the "contamination" accusation, Taylor replied, "I don't see how I could have known the dog was going to be part of a murder investigation. That's what it is isn't it? Murder? He couldn't have hurt himself that way, could he?"

"See you later," was Andrew's curt reply. He turned on his heel and went back to the scene. Andrew at work was a much different proposition from Andrew relaxed in her living room.

Taylor tugged at the cord and the dog stood. He looked back at the truck with a forlorn face and then followed Taylor, head lowered, lead rope loose, moving with a mechanical step.

Edie was waiting for her when they arrived at the kennel. Wisely she hadn't brought her own dog, Jasper, with her.

"Tristan has been barking," she said as she took the lead from Taylor.

"I'll check on him in a minute. Andrew says to put this fellow in a separate kennel and not to wash him or touch him either if you can help it."

"I thought it was something pretty serious," said Edie. "I

heard the sirens. I'll put him in a kennel and make sure he has water for now. Then you can tell me all about it."

"I'll let Tristan out in the back yard for a pee and put the kettle on," said Taylor.

Tristan was more excited than he usually was, which is saying a lot for a Jack Russell. He danced around the back yard, stopping to sniff at the two raised flower beds ringed with stone and then making a circuit of the fence and shrubs that formed three sides of the garden. Apparently deciding everything was as it should be he ran to the gate to investigate the outside, jumping nearly high enough to escape. He knew there was a strange dog there, and he could sense the excitement. He wanted to be part of it. It took some time to get him calmed down enough to do his business and by the time they got inside, the kettle was boiling. Taylor poured it into the teapot and a few seconds later, Edie was at her door.

Edie became Taylor's friend and ally when Taylor moved back to Badger Lake the year earlier. Taylor's Aunt Grace had died and left Taylor the house she had been raised in, but the adjoining lot with the kennel she had left to Edie. In all the years Taylor had lived with Aunt Grace, she knew Edie was her closest friend but never suspected the depth or nature of their relationship. Children are too wrapped up in their own problems to wonder about the love life of their elder family members.

Unravelling a decades old mystery involving Taylor's brother Greg and finding a murderer in their midst had further cemented her friendship with Edie.

Taylor set the teapot in the centre of the kitchen table and slid into the booth that formed seating along one wall. Edie took her usual chair on the opposite side. Taylor was planning to renovate the old house, but couldn't quite bring herself to make the changes. The house was still too full of memories of her brother Greg and of Aunt Grace. Someday she would open it up more. Now, the kitchen was a separate entity with a frosted glass door that shut it off from the rest of the house.

It was handy, sometimes, to keep her pets in or out of areas of the house, but she would prefer a more open concept. And of course the old rounded white fridge was from a different era. The stove was newer, out of necessity, as the oven had given up the ghost months ago. The cupboards too had seen better days, listing along with the house so that some of the doors didn't close properly. She should just go ahead and completely gut the kitchen and refit it. She would someday but for now, it kept alive her childhood memories and she needed to hang onto them for a little longer.

Taylor poured her cup first, not a breach of manners, merely an acknowledgment of different tastes in tea. Edie liked hers extra strong and Taylor preferred a much weaker cup.

Taylor picked up one of the cookies she'd set on a plate. They were store bought ones, but good, vanilla flavoured with a lemon centre. Edie hung her cane over the edge of her chair arm and settled in comfortably. She always carried a cane, but Taylor had never seen her really use it. She could get around quite nicely for a sixty something year old woman and only showed signs of a slight limp when she was tired.

"I got Monty in a kennel by himself but I've never seen a more dejected looking dog." Edie said.

"Monty? I've seen him around often in the truck with Jonah, but never knew his name. Tristan used to bark at him, probably because he was always in the truck and he never had a chance to greet him."

Taylor looked away for a moment before starting, "Jonah's dead," she said. "I found him in the nuisance grounds."

Edie's face showed appropriate shock but no display of grief. "So start from the beginning. How did you come to find Jonah?"

"It was Monty. I heard him howling and barking in front of the kennel. I'm surprised everyone didn't hear him. Anyhow, he made it quite clear that he wanted me to follow him, so I grabbed my phone and did just that. He led me to the nuisance grounds and at first I thought there was a pile of old clothes or garbage lying beside the truck. Then I got close enough to see it was Jonah." She shivered as she recalled her first glimpse of Jonah and the realization he was dead. "I was glad I'd gone back to get my phone."

Taylor stopped to cup her mug of tea and decided it was cool enough to take a sip. Then she went on, "I felt his neck but couldn't find a pulse. I was pretty sure he was dead. There was blood along where his head lay. I knelt down when I checked him so I imagine Andrew will take issue with that, but I had to be sure whether he was alive or not."

"Andrew will understand."

"Hmph. Andrew hasn't been so understanding lately. He's been acting a little weird, as though he has something else on his mind."

"He will. With a murder on his doorstep."

"No, the weird part started before this. He's been a little distracted for a couple of weeks now."

"I'm sure he'll tell you what's bothering him eventually. Andrew has never been a dissembler. So, back to Jonah. Did Andrew say how he died?"

"No, he didn't say anything. It looked like Jonah was hit on the head. I didn't see a knife or gun around. Come to think of it, I didn't see anything he could have been hit on the head with, either." Taylor pushed the cookie around on her plate and heard a distinct rumble coming from her stomach. Of course, she hadn't even had dinner. No wonder she was feeling hunger pangs. She thought her mind might fight with her stomach over the necessity of dinner. She didn't feel much like eating tonight. Not with the picture of Jonah imprinted on her brain.

"Do you think Monty might help the police?" asked Edie.

"Andrew said someone from forensics would want to look at him, especially since he had blood on his muzzle, but I don't see what they could learn from that."

"No, I meant would Monty act strangely if confronted with whoever killed Jonah."

"Oh yes, like Tristan growled at the person who broke into the house and kicked him last summer?"

"Something like that." said Edie.

"I wonder. Monty was locked in the truck when it happened and I'm sure the dump is full of scents belonging to everyone in town. Would he be able to isolate the right one?"

"Probably not. It was just a thought."

"Besides, I think Monty used to bark at everyone that came near the truck. It would be hard to tell..."

A loud knock on the front door interrupted them. "That will be Andrew," said Taylor and ran to let him in. He stepped over the threshold, his tall frame filling the living room. He always looked so much bigger in uniform.

"We were having tea in the kitchen. Would you like some?"

"Maybe a cup wouldn't hurt. But first, I need to get the key for the kennel from Edie. I have someone to look at the dog."

Andrew followed Taylor into the kitchen. Edie had heard the conversation and fished a key out from her pocket. Andrew took it from her and said, "Pour me a cup. I'll be right back."

He returned in a minute or two and sat at the end of the table closest to the door, the one with the view of the street. He added sugar and milk which Taylor set out while he was gone. Neither she nor Edie usually added anything to their tea although on occasion Taylor added milk to thin out Edie's strong brew.

Tristan came over to Andrew for a welcome pat, maybe in hopes of a treat as well. He considered Andrew to be family, just like Edie. Andrew obliged by rubbing him behind the ears. Tristan wriggled with delight and lay down on the floor across Andrew's boots.

Taylor waited impatiently for Andrew to speak, but he stirred the milk and sugar into his tea with maddening deliberation. Finally he leaned back in his chair and said, "So tell me, Taylor, why you?"

"What do you mean, why me? I told you, the dog came here and stood outside the kennel howling. What was I supposed to do, ignore him?"

"That's not exactly what I meant."

Taylor knew what he meant but decided to ignore the unspoken accusation that she had a tendency to find herself in the middle of trouble. That was how she had first met Andrew, in the middle of trouble.

"It was obvious he wanted me to follow him, so I did. I imagine he came here because it is the street closest and the kennel is the first building after the corner."

Andrew grunted and brought his chair down on all fours with a thud. "Did you see or hear anyone while you were there?"

"No. The guy who is usually on the gate would have gone home. But then, once I spotted Jonah, I don't think I would have noticed a clown in drag if I'd seen one. I was floored at the sight of him lying there. I thought at first he might just be hurt so I knelt down and checked to see if I could find a pulse"

"The doctor thinks he was dead for an hour before we got there, which means you didn't miss it by much He'll have a better idea after the autopsy. It probably took the dog a while to get out of the truck. The door is all chewed up where he was clawing at it to get out."

"Poor thing," said Edie. "Once your man—,"

"Woman, actually," interrupted Andrew.

"Once your woman is done, shall I keep Monty in the kennel? I don't think Jonah has anyone close enough to take him. What will happen to him?"

"It's too soon to know anything, but I'd appreciate it if you'd keep him until we know what to do with him."

"How long have you known Jonah?" This question was directed at Edie, who had been a resident of Badger Lake all her life and taught about half the other residents. "Since he came to town? I hear he's been around about four years."

"Oh long before that," said Edie. "He's been here for four years this time, but he grew up in Badger Lake. He was away for ages. No one knew where. Then he suddenly turned up again."

"I didn't know that. Does he have any family around?"

"Only his father. But he won't know anything. He's been in the Care Home for years."

"Is that why Jonah came back to town? To be near his father?"

Edie snorted. "Not a chance. His father was a miserable old so and so. Used to drink hard and then came home and took out his problems on his wife and kids."

"Kids?"

"Yes, Jonah has a sister somewhere. She's a year or so older than him. Anna, that was her name. I taught both of them for a time."

"Do you know where she is?"

"No idea. She left town as soon as she could get away. She doesn't come back to visit."

"What happened to the mother?"

"She died years ago. I think she had cancer. Anna had already left town. I think Jonah hung around long enough to take care of her. When she died, he was gone too."

"Well," said Andrew. He got up, setting down the empty cup as he stood and pushing the chair under the table. "I'll have to stop in at the Care Home and let the father know anyhow. He's still next of kin."

"You won't get much through to him. He's got Alzheimer's. I don't know if he has lucid moments or not."

"I'll talk to someone on staff. Then they can decide what they want me to tell him. I'll have to track down the sister too. I guess you don't know if she's married or not?" This question was directed to Edie.

"Not a clue."

"Taylor, I'll need you to stop off sometime and make a formal statement about finding Jonah. Can you come in tomorrow morning?"

Taylor nodded. A knock came to the door and Andrew said, "That will be for me. She'll be done with the dog. Thanks for the tea. See you tomorrow." Tristan jumped up and followed him to the door. He was still hoping for a treat.

Taylor could hear muffled voices on the step but couldn't make out any words. Then footsteps down the walk and two vehicles heading out.

The silence filled the room. Andrew had a presence that left a hole when he went.

Edie said, "I'd better be going home too. It's been a stressful day for you." She took her cup to the sink and retrieved her cane from the arm of the chair. "Let me know if you hear anything new from the station when you go to make your statement."

"I don't imagine they'll tell me anything but I'll keep my ears open."

When Edie had gone, Taylor fed an impatient Tristan and opened a can for Denver. He had materialized from out of nowhere at her feet.

She opened the fridge door and stared into it but could see nothing that appealed to her. She checked the freezer and pulled out a chicken and rice frozen dinner. It would have to do. A partial bottle of white wine called to her from the fridge door rack and she poured a liberal glass as the frozen dinner nuked.

Taylor settled in the recliner, wine glass to the side and

meal on her knee. She flicked on the television but out of all those channels, nothing looked interesting to her. She needed a distraction and some noise so she finally chose a stand-up comedy program. She could use a few laughs tonight.

She soon found out eating in the living room was not a good idea. First Tristan stood at her feet looking soulfully at her, head cocked to the side, a picture of longing and hunger. Next Denver hopped on the couch, from there to the side table and then to the back of her chair. Feeling surrounded, she gave up and returned to the kitchen table to finish. The comedy show had nothing on her pets for humour.

She called it an early night and was in bed by ten o'clock. Sleeping was another matter. Giving up after an hour of rolling from side to side of the bed, she snapped on the nightstand light and picked through the stash of books she had. Most of them she ruled out. She wasn't in the mood for mystery and Andrew's strange behaviour of late was cooling her taste for romance. She opened instead, a biography, and was soon in an African jungle with a group of chimpanzees and Jane Goodall.

Chapter
Four

Morning came with a start, as Taylor surfaced from a dream. The dream somehow tangled together the troubles of yesterday with her night time reading. A group of chimpanzees were driving Jonah's truck and canvassing the town looking for odd jobs. Who needs sit-coms? She could dream her own.

Denver sat on her pillow looking serene but she knew it was a pose. He had probably been responsible for her quick awakening, darting a paw at her face and then assuming innocence. Tristan was at her bedside, ready to start his morning whimper for attention.

She got up and looked after her roommates first. Then she turned on the coffee and headed for the shower.

She decided to go to the RCMP station first thing after breakfast and make her statement. Best to get it over with.

She left the car at home and walked, combining Tristan's exercise with her errand. *They won't mind Tristan coming to the station. They all know him.*

Miranda, the middle-aged blonde at the front desk, seemed to be expecting her and led her into a small room. She stooped to pat Tristan and a dog treat materialized from her desk. "Andrew said to write it down as it happened. He said just the facts. No need to be fanciful or give opinions. Then we'll type it up and you can sign it."

Taylor bristled at the instructions Andrew felt he had to leave. She bet he didn't put it that way for other witnesses.

She looked around and could see no sign of him. Miranda was the only one besides her. She took about ten minutes to write down what had happened. She made it plain and simple, as requested. *It's his fault if I missed something.* The first time he asked her to expand on her statement, she'd tell him so too.

Miranda read and typed the statement. She smiled as though she were enjoying it. A quick signature, a second treat for Tristan, and Taylor was on her way home. Certainly nothing new to be learned here.

She was a block away from home when she met Edie heading downtown.

"Going shopping?" Then she noticed Edie carried no shopping bag, nothing but her cane.

"No. Going for my usual morning round of coffee and gossip at the Northland. Want to come?"

"Just give me a minute to drop off Tristan and I'll join you."

She quickly walked the last short block to her house, put Tristan inside and shut the door behind her, ignoring the pleas from her dog that he wasn't finished his walk yet. Then she joined Edie. She took a quick look at her watch. "A little earlier than usual today, aren't you?"

"The Northland is going to be full today." said Edie. "Everyone will be full of gossip, so I figured I'd come early to be sure to get a table."

She was right. Taylor blinked to accustom her eyes to the darker interior and looked around. Most tables were already full and a steady hum of conversation filled the air. It stopped for a second when she and Edie walked in. She knew it wasn't just a check to see who the new coffee seekers were. Everyone probably knew she had been the one to find Jonah.

Edie was already on her way to the only booth still empty. Taylor followed her and Jean, the waitress, was at their table immediately with a carafe of hot coffee.

The conversations had resumed but Taylor could feel without seeing, the glances sent her way. She felt a little shudder as she remembered a similar situation last year. Taylor had recently arrived back in Badger Lake when she was caught up in a mystery that ended in two deaths and nearly a third—her own.

Now here she was back in the centre of things, a fact she was sure everyone in the coffee shop had already noted. She was starting to feel like Typhoid Mary, bringing destruction by her mere presence.

"Did you notice," said Edie, "There's a lot of chatter about Jonah but I don't see a sense of loss on anyone's face."

"You're right," agreed Taylor. "It's so sad, isn't it, not to have anyone to mourn your death, especially a violent death like this. I wonder if Andrew will find the sister. Didn't Jonah have any friends? After all, he's been here four years."

"Probably has a few acquaintances that hung out in the pub, but I doubt he ever got close to anyone. From what I remember of Jonah he was damaged goods from a young age."

"Yet he stayed to look after his mother when she was ill. And he seems to have carved out a life and a business here. He can't be that damaged."

"Jonah was always good at putting on a face. That much hasn't changed. But I don't think he was a very nice man. And I can think of quite a few people in town who would agree."

Taylor gave Edie a questioning look but she shook her head. "I'll tell you about it later."

The coffee shop door opened again and a well—dressed couple looked around searching for a seat. They spotted Taylor and Edie and crossed the room to their booth. "Okay if we join you? It's a bit crowded this morning. Not a surprise I guess."

"Of course, Reverend. Please sit down."

"Thanks. And call me Steven, please. We try to keep the formality down outside of church. After all, we're one community here."

The couple who had joined them was Steven and Brenda Prentiss, United Church minister and his wife.

Neither Edie or Taylor were regular churchgoers but when Taylor did go to a service, it was at the United. She liked Steven Prentiss. His sermons tended to be based less on Biblical references than on everyday issues facing people. Taylor even went so far as to join the UCW when invited by the rather strong minded Agnes Walker, pillar of the church and town. It wasn't something she really wanted to do, but she felt a pressure to join since she went to the church. After all, she should do at least one thing to support her community.

Taylor wasn't so sure how she felt about Brenda. She met her at the occasional UCW meeting she felt obliged to attend, but she always felt Brenda was one of those people who left unsaid more than she said. You were left to fill in the blanks. She couldn't see any harm in her though. Maybe she only learned to be close—mouthed because of her position as minister's wife. She must hear a lot of things she couldn't talk about. Maybe she found it safest not to say much at all. Taylor didn't envy her the position.

Steven waited for his wife to be seated before taking the outside spot on the bench. Brenda sat carefully, smoothing the skirt of her patterned tan dress and adjusting the cuffs on both sleeves before looking up to add her greeting.

"I hear you were the one to find Jonah?" Rev. Prentiss, (Taylor was going to have problems with calling him Steven), formed it as a question rather than a statement.

"Yes," said Taylor simply, not sure how much she should reveal, but then decided if you couldn't confide in your minister, who could you trust?

"It was his dog, actually," she added.

"Monty?" This from Brenda. Taylor remembered she was a dog person. She had two of her own. Taylor had occasionally met Brenda out for walks and Tristan seemed to approve of the dogs after the initial circling and sniffing tests were complete. Brenda had struck her as an unusual dog lover, given her outwardly fastidious behaviour. It was hard to imagine her accepting doggie kisses and brushing dog hair from her clothing. But then, her dogs were miniature poodles so wouldn't be shedders.

"I heard him howling and barking outside Edie's kennel. When I went to see what the trouble was, he insisted, sort of Lassie style, that I follow him. So I did. He led me to the garbage dump and there was Jonah beside his truck. I called the police and ambulance. End of story. Or at least my part in it," she added firmly.

"The police may have a hard time sorting out suspects," said Brenda, "Jonah had a lot of enemies, or at least people who didn't like him. A few men in town will be happy to see the end of him." It seemed a slightly unchristian attitude from a minister's wife and Taylor could see a sideways glance of disapproval from Steven aimed at his wife.

Brenda ignored the glance and went on. "It's too bad he ever came back to Badger Lake. I wonder why he did." Brenda seemed in the mood to step out of her mould as the reticent minister's wife.

Taylor was aware the conversation around their table had hushed and she could almost feel the ears twitching. She was dying to change the subject but couldn't think of a way to get off topic.

Edie came to the rescue. "Are you still looking for donations for the Bake Sale on Saturday?" she asked Brenda.

Brenda gave a little jump and looked around questioningly as though she had missed something. Taylor thought her mind seemed fixed on Jonah and she wasn't ready to move the conversation on.

Brenda must have realized the question needed an answer because she smiled over-brightly and said. "Anything you can do to help would be greatly appreciated Edie. Your cinnamon buns and breads are famous."

Steven and Edie managed to keep the conversation on clerical and community lines. Taylor joined in and Brenda added a comment of two. She had relapsed into her taciturn mode. The hum of words grew again at the nearby tables.

The coffee crew slowly thinned out of the Northland and Edie made a move to go. "It's time I checked on Jasper and Monty," she said.

Steven insisted on picking up the coffee tab so Edie and Taylor bid their thanks and farewells and walked together in the direction of their homes.

"Thanks for getting me off the hook," said Taylor. "I'm sorry you got coerced into the baking, though."

"Oh, I was planning to do the buns and bread anyway. I always do. Brenda knows that."

"Are you going to come in for another cup of coffee and tell me what you know about Jonah?"

"We'll go to my place instead, if that's all right."

They walked down the back lane that separated Taylor's street from Edie's and kept a comfortable silence until they were inside, seated in Edie's neat and welcoming kitchen.

Edie put the kettle on. "Tea okay? I've had my fill of coffee for the day."

"Fine with me." Taylor could smell the cinnamon buns before Edie set the plates on the table. "Tea at your house is so much better than mine. I'll never make a good cook. I volunteered to man a table and the cash drawer at the sale just so I didn't have to inflict my baking on anyone." She thought a moment and said. "I notice I didn't get an argument from the others. They had a sampling of my skills last sale. I think I took home nearly as much as I brought."

Edie didn't reply or offer any disclaimer, seemingly lost in her own thoughts. She poured Taylor's tea and gave the pot a swirl, setting it down, waiting till it was Edie—strength before pouring her own.

Taylor pulled a strip of gooey sugary dough from the bun and popped it into her mouth, closing her eyes in delight. Edie's buns were to die for. They were extra buttery and brown-sugary and she had the good sense not to ruin them with frosting.

Two more mouthfuls and she decided the time had come.

"All right, give," she said. "What do you know about Jonah that I don't? And is it something we should pass on to Andrew?"

Edie considered a moment before she spoke. "I plan to talk to Andrew later. I'll give him the general gist of what I'm about to tell you."

She pushed her plate with the cinnamon bun to the side and cupped her tea mug with her hands.

"I told you Jonah was not a nice person. I found out personally a couple of years ago when he did some work for me."

"Didn't finish the job or do the work properly?"

"Nothing like that. Actually he was very good at what he did. No, it was after the work was done and I was about to pay him the amount he quoted. Suddenly he upped the amount. I told him that wasn't the agreed price and he began to talk about my relationship with your Aunt Grace."

"He didn't!"

"Grace came over here often and I guess while he was working here he must have put two and two together and worked out what our relationship was."

"But you would never give in to blackmail!"

"Of course not. Jonah thought in a small town, I might not want people to know our relationship. I told him he could tell whomever he wanted, that the town already knew and didn't care."

"How did he react to that?"

"He backed down pretty quickly, said that's not what he meant at all and went back to the original quote."

"So," said Taylor slowly. "If he tried it on with you, there may be others in town he tried it on. And other people might have cared more than you about their personal lives being known."

"I should have paid more attention to him after that. But how could I warn people? I couldn't very well take out an ad in the paper and say Jonah tried to blackmail me. Hide your secrets."

"If you tell Andrew, I imagine it will give him a line to follow. Other than that, who would want to kill him? He always seemed a friendly fellow and yet..."

"And yet what?"

"Did you notice at the coffee shop, it was so different from last year when Jennie and Tara Lynn died. Everyone was shocked then and maybe gossiped a lot, but they were genuinely sorry. You could see it in their faces."

Edie finished her thought. "But with Jonah, it was no more than conversation about something that happened in town, there was no grief in anyone's voices."

"Sad, isn't it? I wonder if Andrew will track down the sister. Or if she'll even care either."

"She might. It was the father she ran away from, not Jonah."

"But what about Brenda's comment about the men happy to see the back of him? Sounds like there must be at least one or two women in town who might mourn him. If it's true, that is."

Edie frowned a little and said. "If he did have a romantic interest, it was probably with a married woman," she said. "I've never seen him around town in the company of a anyone, so he's been pretty discreet about his relationships. Of course I'm not out on the town, but I'm sure I'd know if he was seeing someone in the open."

"I wonder how Brenda knows."

"Minister's wife?'

"Yes, her husband gave her a look after she made that comment. She probably knows a lot about people she can't divulge. So does he, of course."

"I know before Jonah went away, he left a trail of affairs behind him. Of course none of that would matter now. And he wasn't so circumspect then, so everyone knew who he was going with."

Taylor wasn't so sure it wouldn't matter. She knew from experience old history could spring up when least expected.

She went back to her cinnamon bun, but not with as much enjoyment as when she started. She tried to picture Jonah riding along in his pickup, dog riding shotgun, and couldn't reconcile that with the person she now knew he was.

"There's one person who will miss him," Taylor said. "Monty."

"Speaking of Monty, I had better go and look after him. Not that he'll likely eat anything. Maybe if I take Jasper along, he can do some dog therapy." Jasper acknowledged the mention of his name with a serious tail wagging and stood up beside Edie, ready for whatever adventure or chore she was going to give him.

Chapter Five

Taylor wasn't ready for lunch yet after the huge cinnamon bun she had at Edie's so she opted for exercise instead, to burn off the calories. Tristan seconded her choice. He was always ready for a walk. The short trip to the police station earlier didn't qualify in his opinion.

She wandered along the residential streets, avoiding the downtown, and soon was in the east end by the motel and the huge new United Church. She saw a familiar figure coming towards her attached by a leash to a little black and white mixed breed dog whose tail began wagging furiously when he saw Tristan. Taylor had gone to high school with Darcy and she was one of the few old friends she had kept in contact with during the years she was away. That was down to Darcy, not her. Taylor had all but washed the dirt of Badger Lake from her feet when she left, except for Aunt Grace, of course. It was Darcy who refused to let the miles come between them and she kept had up a chain of letters and e-mails.

"Hi Darcy. Hi Bruno." Taylor stooped to give the little dog a pat, but he didn't stand still. He and Tristan were busy with the circling and sniffing that formed dog greeting protocol.

"Did you hear about Jonah?" asked Darcy. The she quickly put her free hand over her mouth. "Oh, I'm sorry, of course you did. Jillian at the motel said it was you who found him. That must have been awful."

"It was awful. I hope I never have to see a dead body again."

"I'm ready for a coffee. How about you? You haven't seen our new house yet, have you? Dan was so pleased we could buy the old Trent house. His family rented that house when they first moved to Badger Lake. Why don't you come in and have a visit? It's closer than the burger joint and I don't think the burger place would let us bring the dogs in anyhow."

"Between The Northland and Edie, I'm overfull of coffee and tea, but I'd love to see what you're doing to your house."

"You might have to walk over debris and chunks of drywall on the way in. We're going to be in Reno mode for a while, I'm afraid, since we're doing it ourselves. I just hope we get it done before..." Darcy gave a little smile that Taylor would have described as a 'cat that swallowed the canary' look.

Taylor interpreted the look and stopped in her tracks. "You're not!"

"I am." said Darcy, "But just. We told our respective parents about it yesterday, so I imagine it will be public any minute now."

Taylor leaned over and gave Darcy a hug. "I'm so happy for you," she said. "I imagine Dan is thrilled."

"Bursting his suspenders, if he wore suspenders that is."

They walked down the back lane to the rear entrance of Darcy's house and came in through a back garden that was lined with flower beds. The beds sported a few blooms mixed with some dead stalks and more than a few weeds. Taylor guessed the renovations, or reno, was a full time operation and had second thoughts about the plans she had considered for her house.

The kitchen was prepped for the changes, with cupboard doors taken off their hinges and old wallpaper sticking out of the top of an industrial sized garbage bag in the corner of the room. The fridge and stove were pulled out from the wall and counter space was nonexistent.

"The kitchen is first in line," said Darcy. "But we're going to do it all. Once the kitchen and bathroom are done, the rest will follow. No sense in doing half a house. Now," she turned to the overfilled countertops. "I think I might just find the coffee maker somewhere." Taylor was going to decline as she was already floating away, but somehow, one always had room for another cup of coffee.

They shooed the dogs out in the fenced back yard to play. Luckily they got along well together.

"So, tell me about the baby. Have you been to the doctor yet, or just done the home test?"

"I had my appointment earlier this week. I wanted it confirmed by Dr. Jeffries before we told our parents. She said everything looks good."

"Do you know if it's going to be a boy or a girl?"

"Dan and I have been talking about that. I don't think we want to know ahead of time. It will be more fun to be surprised."

"But if you're renovating? It might be easier to decorate the baby's room?"

Darcy brought the coffee pot over. "I thought of that. We might change our minds later, when we get into paint colours but for now, we're just happy I'm pregnant. The rest can wait."

Darcy poured two mugs of coffee and put the pot back on the burner. "Now," she said as she pulled out a chair opposite Taylor. "Let's get to the topic of conversation that's got everyone gossiping. How did you come to be the one to find Jonah?"

Taylor explained about the appearance of Monty and her follow up. It wasn't the same chore repeating the story to Darcy that it was to the Prentiss couple. It was always better to talk about unpleasant things to a friend.

"I don't imagine Andrew was pleased to have you involved in another of his investigations."

"I honestly don't know what's running through Andrew's mind these days, Darcy. He's been acting rather strange."

"Strange how?"

"The only way I can describe it is hot and cold. Sometimes he seems like the old Andrew—when we're out for dinner or just hanging out with friends. Then every so often, he gets this faraway look and seems to forget I'm even in the room. I thought for a while it might be another woman in his life, but..."

"But that doesn't sound like Andrew." finished Darcy. "If he had someone else in his life, he would be up front about it. Besides, in Badger Lake someone would have seen him and started talking about it. I'm sure you have nothing to worry about." Then Darcy brightened . "Hey, maybe he's trying to decide whether to pop the question and hasn't worked up the nerve yet."

Taylor laughed at the idea. "I don't think we've reached that point yet," she said. But the suggestion stopped her cold for a moment. How would she feel if that was the idea Andrew had on his mind? *Ridiculous.* Neither she nor Andrew was ready for that.

She changed the subject. "Did Dan know Jonah?' she asked. "They must have worked together sometimes if Dan was doing electrical work when Jonah did his carpentry."

"Not often," said Darcy. "But I know someone who knew him—rather too well." Her face became somber.

"Who?"

"I don't know if you remember the Limbaughs? Danika was a couple of years ahead of us in school. Probably more Greg's age."

"I recognize the name but can't really picture her. I forgot a lot about Badger Lake in the years I was away."

Darcy reached over and gave her hand a reassuring pat. "Well, Danika stayed in Badger Lake and used to work at the insurance office with me. I think she's at the dental clinic now. You probably saw her there but didn't remember her. She began seeing Jonah when she got out of school."

"He would be a lot older than her?"

"A few years. Not enough to be a big issue. Anyhow, she got pregnant and the minute it became news, Jonah dropped her like a hot potato. This was right after his mother died. He took off out of town—maybe he was leaving anyhow. Nobody saw him until a few years ago when he suddenly turned up."

"So what about Danika?"

"She had the baby and raised it by herself. If Jonah had stayed in town, she probably would have pushed the support issue, but since he disappeared, she had no way to find him. She lived with her parents and raised Franny herself. Franny's probably," Darcy wrinkled her brow, figuring years on her head, "She's probably eleven or twelve now."

"I wonder why Danika didn't go after Jonah for support when he came back to town."

"She did. At least I think she did at first. Then she

seemed to give up the idea.. Maybe she had her life in order and didn't want it changed. If it were me, I'd rather skip the support payments and leave Jonah out of my kid's life."

"Strange man not wanting to acknowledge his daughter."

"Life is full of strange men. I'm glad I got one of the not so strange ones. You too." she smiled at Taylor. "Andrew is one of the good ones. Hang onto him."

"I'm not going to hang onto him if he doesn't want to be held on to. And lately I'm not so sure. Oh well, let's talk about something else. Back to Jonah."

"I think there are a few more people in town not sorry to see him dead. Oh, that's a horrible thing to say. I didn't really mean it."

"But—if someone in town had to die, the consensus is that better Jonah than anyone else?"

"Something like that."

"That's the feeling I got in the Northland over coffee this morning. But why did no one like him? It can't be because he's a deadbeat dad. There must be more to it than that."

"Must be. No one gives any reasons. They just didn't like him. And then too, he had a string of badly ended romances. Remember, he went out with Kelly before she married Hank?"

"I don't think I was in Badger Lake then. Looks like Kelly upgraded marrying Hank."

Taylor thought back to the story Edie had told and wondered if Jonah's blackmailing attempt could be at the root of it. If he tried it on Edie, he surely tried it on others. As a handyman, he probably had a good chance while having the run of a house, to root out secrets.

"Your mind is off somewhere," said Darcy. "Give."

"Well, I was thinking about reasons people have to dislike a person." Taylor approached the conversation slowly. She didn't want to tell Edie's secret, but then it wasn't a secret. She went on. "Did you ever wonder if Jonah pried too much into people's lives and then tried to take advantage of it?"

"Blackmailing you mean?"

That was the word Taylor was trying to avoid, but she nodded. "Yes."

"I wouldn't be surprised. It sounds in character. Do you have reason to suspect that's what he was doing?"

"Not really," Taylor lied. "It just sounds like a good way to make enemies."

"Hmmm." said Darcy. "I wonder..."

"Wonder what?"

"Nothing. Would you like another cup?" She gestured with the pot.

Taylor declined. "No thanks, I've had too much coffee already today. Between that and Edie's strong tea, I'll be hanging from the chandelier for the rest of the day. I'd better get home and try to do some work while I still have the coffee buzz."

She went to the back door and called Tristan who played hard to get before finally heeding her call. He was having too much fun to want to leave his friend.

"Why don't you and Dan come over for dinner one night this week?" Taylor asked. "It will save you a day of cooking and dishwashing which must be difficult. I'll see if Andrew is free—he can't spend all his waking hours working on the case—and we can have a lasagna night with a movie."

"Sounds good to me. Let me know what night is good for Andrew. Any night that gets me out of this kitchen works for me. And Dan too," she added.

Tristan protested a moment when she snapped his leash on but then trotted dutifully beside Taylor on the way home. The play date must have done him good. He didn't pull at his leash every time they came to a crossroad the way he often did. Tristan preferred the less travelled byways of life.

Taylor checked Denver's box and water dish before settling down to work. Denver and Tristan followed her into the section of living room she used as an office more than she did the upstairs one she'd created in the spare bedroom. She still liked her desktop upstairs but for short bursts of work, she appreciated the portability of her laptop. Tristan plopped down at her feet and Denver looked up at her expectantly until she cleared a spot on the chair beside her for him to jump up to. Bad mistake. Once Denver was on her knee, he positioned himself between Taylor and the keyboard. It took about five minutes of devoted petting before he would settle down beside her and let her work. The computer keyboard was one of his favourite places.

Taylor had a late lunch and indulged herself afterwards

with a rare treat. She lay down on the couch, dog and cat jockeying for space beside her, and dozed off.

It didn't last long. Twenty minutes later she was awake but feeling much fresher than before her nap. I must be reaching middle—age a little early, she thought. I shouldn't be having afternoon naps. She spent the next two hours at her computer catching up on work and correspondence. Then she looked at her watch and realized she hadn't taken anything out for dinner. She could always nuke another frozen dinner but she wanted something fresh so she took her green bags and headed for the store.

"Sorry Tristan, You wouldn't be very welcome in the grocery aisles." She walked out into a late afternoon sun that heated the cloudless day past the point of comfort. The morning breeze that made her earlier walk pleasant was now stifled. She glanced at the car but knew it would be much hotter inside it and the air conditioning would just start to work about the time she got home. The steering wheel would be blisteringly hot. She should invest in a garage, she thought, or at least a carport when she got into her renos. Not only for shade in the summer but to keep the ice and snow off in winter.

Taylor picked up some greens, peppers of varying colors, and some nuts and dried fruit. She would cook the chicken after all, she thought and add it to the salad. Good dinner plan for a warm day. Maybe some iced tea to go along with it. On the way to the check-out she passed the cooler of single sized drinks. She normally tried to stay away from soft drinks but the cola called to her and she picked one up.

'Hi Taylor, I hear you had an exciting day yesterday." Kelly, the cashier, was another face from her past. She was one of the few girls from Taylor's class that had stayed in Badger Lake. Kelly's long brown hair hung down her back in a single braid. She was tall and well—endowed. Her uniform shirt fitted her in a way Taylor envied. Kelly had always been one of the more popular girls in their class, never at a loss for dates. She had left them all open—mouthed when she slipped off for a weekend to marry a widower more than a decade older than her with two little boys. No—one had seen that romance coming, but all conceded that Hank was lucky to have found a mother for his boys. Taylor hadn't been in town then, but Aunt Grace and Darcy had kept her up to date on weddings and funerals. She remembered Darcy's morning tidbit about Jonah and Kelly. That part had been left out of her updates.

Kelly's family had now expanded to include a set of twins born, some busybodies commented, with unseemly haste after the wedding. Her husband seemed devoted to her. Maybe a little too devoted, was the local opinion. But that's what you would expect when a man married a woman that much younger.

"It was excitement I could do without," Taylor answered. "I just hope the police find out soon who did it."

"Well, they'll be spoiled for choice," said Kelly, scanning the items in Taylor's basket as she talked. Her face clouded as she leaned over to speak softly, an unnecessary move, since the store was nearly deserted and no one else stood in line.

"I've heard he wasn't, well-liked," said Taylor, "but not liking someone doesn't usually lead to murder."

"It's not a matter of liking." said Kelly sotto voice. "I think Jonah put his nose into people's affairs once too often."

"Do you have anyone in particular in mind?"

"I have my suspicions in a couple of cases, but nothing I know for sure. If I knew for sure, then so would everyone else and there's be no point in shutting Jonah up."

"Is that what you think happened?" Taylor inserted her debit card into the machine to pay for her groceries.

"I wouldn't be surprised." Kelly's gaze lingered suggestively and Taylor felt as though Kelly were trying to tell her something beyond her words. But then, if she and Jonah were once an item, as Darcy said, maybe she had some resentment left.

Kelly passed the till receipt to her and suddenly stiffened. Taylor followed her gaze to the entrance where Kelly's husband Hank stood. When she shifted her gaze back to Kelly she was looking at her husband with a wide smile. Had she imagined Kelly's first reaction to her husband's appearance? Strangely, Hank gave a grimace of a smile in return, waved quickly at Taylor, and disappeared out the door. Sometimes Taylor had envied Kelly her seemingly happy marriage and family of boys. But now she wasn't so sure. Was there trouble in paradise?

Taylor walked home deep in thought. Everyone seemed to be of one mind regarding Jonah. No one liked him. Everybody thought he meddled—translate to blackmailed—but no one had anything definite to go on and no one named names. Andrew was going to have lots of fun trying to get information out of this crowd. Taylor intended to stay right out of it. No one was going to drag her into trouble this time, just because she had found the body.

She unpacked her bags, holding them high until she could put them on the counter, away from the sniffing noses of her pets. "There's nothing in here for you," she said, "Unless you've both suddenly developed a taste for salad."

They soon decided nothing of interest was in the bags and instead moved to their food dishes, making a strong hint.

"Too early for supper." said Taylor. "Tristan, I'm too hot and tired for another walk so you can go play in the back yard for a while. Get your business done and then we'll talk about supper."

She put a chicken breast in the mic on defrost and began putting her salad together. When the chicken was thawed enough to cut into slices she pulled out the frying pan and began to brown them.

Denver kept up a steady circling of her legs. Salad might not be his thing, but chicken certainly was.

She called Andrew while the chicken was cooking. The idea of a dinner with him and Darcy and Dan sounded just the thing to banish thoughts of Jonah.

He answered right away but with a quick," Can't talk now, I'm in the middle of something, Taylor. I'll call you back in about an hour." He hung up without a goodbye, not an unusual move for Andrew, especially if someone else was with him, but it added to Taylor's concerns about the growing rift in their friendship.

She shrugged and decided an early supper was in the cards for tonight. Calling Tristan in from the yard, she fed him and Denver and made her salad. The cold cola went down to the halfway point in a couple of big gulps. She usually ate at the kitchen table, a necessity with pets, but tonight she closed the kitchen door on them as they finished their own meals and took her into the living room in front of the television.

She finished the last of her chicken salad and was about to take her plate to the kitchen when she heard someone at the front door. She recognized Andrew's staccato knock, and set her plate down on the side table, trying not to appear in a hurry as she answered.

Andrew was standing on her step with a big grin and a fistful of dandelions which he presented to her with a flourish. Taylor felt a rush of relief. The old Andrew was back.

"Am I to take it you are comparing me to a bunch of weeds?"

He rubbed his chin as though in consideration. "Sometimes the comparison seems apt," he said, "But for now, let's just say the dandelion is a pretty and much maligned flower."

She took the dandelions and her plate to the kitchen, Andrew following in her wake.

When she pushed open the sliding door that enclosed the kitchen, Tristan and Denver did their usual search of newcomers to see if they were bearing treats. Denver lost interest immediately and headed off for a comfortable bed. Tristan followed Andrew, one of his favorite people, and when Andrew pulled out a kitchen chair and sat, Tristan lay down by his feet, a sure sign of approval.

"You seem to get along with dogs so well," Taylor said. "Why don't you have one of your own?" It was a question aimed at establishing a comfort zone more than a request for information, but it was something she'd wondered about on occasion.

"I did. I had a border collie called Jack. He died just before you moved back last year."

"Oh," said Taylor. "I'm sorry. You've never talked about him."

"Jack was an old dog. I'd had him since I was a teenager. He was already well past his allotted years. Then he got sick and in pain and I had Vivian put him down."

Taylor could have kicked herself for the turn she'd given the conversation. Andrew's good mood had evaporated and she had a sudden chilling thought to the future when Tristan reached that stage. Would she have the courage to put him out of his pain?

"I'm sorry," she said softly. "Have you ever considered getting another dog?"

"Maybe someday," he said. "Now, what can you offer that's cold?" he gave a pointed look at her empty cola glass.

"Last one, I'm afraid," she said. "But I do have iced tea in the fridge. Will that do?"

Knowing the answer, she poured him a glass and set it in front of him along with a plate of cookies, not her usual bought ones, but a plate of chocolate chip home—made cookies Edie had given her.

He dived right in to the cookies and swallowed half his iced tea in one gulp, setting the glass down with a clunk.

"Did you want something in particular earlier, or were you just calling to say hello?"

"I didn't mean to interrupt you." Taylor began thinking the right approach might bring information a direct question wouldn't.

"If that's a way of asking what you interrupted, I'm not going to answer. You are staying right out of this, under- stood?"

"Of course," she said with the most demure expression she could muster. "I have no intention of getting involved. I didn't deliberately find Jonah's body, you know."

"Hmm." he gave her a suspicious glance, well aware that her curiosity sometimes got in the way of common sense.

"The reason I called was to ask you to dinner."

"Tonight? I've already eaten. and so have you, unless you're in the habit of carrying empty plates around the house."

"Not tonight, silly. But some night this week. I want to have Darcy and Dan over and I thought we could have a la- sagna and movie night."

"Sounds good."

"Tomorrow night?"

"Okay. I don't think we're going to get sudden move- ments on this investigation but if we do, I might have to can- cel at the last minute."

"Let's take that chance and make it tomorrow."

He finished the last of the iced tea and began to stand up.

"You're going so soon?"

"If I want to get all my paper work caught up so I can have tomorrow night free for dinner, then yes."

"Um—Andrew?" Taylor wasn't sure how to broach the topic she had in mind.

He stopped, one hand on the door handle and turned, but if anything she had read about body language was true, he wasn't giving her much of an opening. His torso was leaning into the door as though ready to fly out at a moment's notice.

"What?" The word came out short and sharp. Taylor nearly said "Never mind," but took a gulp and went on. "Remember last year when the intruder broke into my house and kicked Tristan?" Was she mistaken or did Andrew suddenly relax? What subject was he trying to avoid that he was afraid she was going to open?

"I'm not likely to forget."

"Remember when I took Tristan for a walk and he barked at Bill?"

"But it wasn't Bill he was actually barking at."

"No, but that was my fault. He was trying to tell me who hurt him. Now, suppose Monty would do the same thing?"

Andrew appeared to consider the idea. Taylor could tell from the movement of his jaw that he was biting his inner cheek, something he often did when lost in thought.

"It's not the craziest idea you've ever had," he said slowly.

"Gee, thanks. Does that mean it's worth a try?"

"Possibly. I'll think about it. Forensics is done with Jonah's truck, so I could come over tomorrow, pick up Monty and take him for a drive. That should get a few stares on Main Street."

Andrew leaned over and gave her a brief kiss, then a quick moment of eye contact accompanied by what could only be described as a chuckle, shook his head, and left.

Taylor wondered if the look he had given her was significant. He appeared to be back to himself, but she had flickering doubts. Their relationship wasn't on firm enough grounds that she could actually come out and ask him what the problem was. But why couldn't she? It was a simple question—'Is something bothering you about us?' She knew she was afraid the answer might not be that simple.

She checked the air flow and moved her fan from one

window to another in the living room. Air conditioning. She should add that to her reno list. The trouble was that the list kept getting bigger and her bank account was staying put. She didn't want to delve into credit card debt to do her changes. Besides, she still had ambivalent feelings about changing her childhood home.

Enough procrastinating and excuses! She had been promising herself to get work done on the house since she had moved in. The sight of Darcy's kitchen chaos was a guilty reminder that she hadn't done a thing in that direction. Tomorrow she would remedy that. She would call—who?

Normally, Jonah would be the first on the list to call. He was the most visible handyman in town, and no matter what people's opinions were of him personally, no one found fault with his work. She didn't want to get a contractor if she could help. Too much money. But if she needed changes to the electrical or plumbing, she'd have to get someone who could submit plans to the town council for approval and who was qualified to implement them.

She wondered if Jimmy who ran the local fix—it shop would do a renovating project. She had called him, or rather Andrew had, last year when she needed a new door and locks changed, but she wasn't sure if his shop left him time for something on a larger scale. It wouldn't hurt to ask him. She would start small—say one room only. But which one? The kitchen was the obvious choice but it was the largest project and she wasn't ready to tackle it yet. She'd opt for the bathroom instead. It had an old—fashioned sink with no storage room and a tiny bath. She'd ask Jimmy what he could do.

If she was going to have someone closely inspecting her bathroom, she knew it needed a deep clean. She changed into old shorts and tank top and, armed with scouring pads and every cleaner she could find, set to the task. When she had finished she stood back and took a look. For all the work she had done, it didn't look a lot better. That confirmed her decision that it needed a sprucing up.

Feeling quite smug about her dedicated cleaning project she felt she was due the reward of a good soak. Lying in bubbles up to her chin, to hide the now obvious scratches and pings on the tub, she lay back and closed her eyes.

Chapter Six

Next morning Taylor had an early breakfast and paid extra attention to her oral cleaning routine, flossing a second round and brushing with a heavier hand than usual. She wasn't looking forward to her dental appointment, but at least it was only a cleaning she had booked. It seemed strange to be so worried about the cleanliness of her teeth on the way to a cleaning, but then why did people de—clutter their house before the housekeeper arrived and wash their car before the trip to the garage? She made a mental note to wash her car. It was due for a service. Then she giggled as she thought how true to form she was reacting. Dental appointments made a person act strangely.

Tristan seemed to recognize her preoccupation and did his business without his normal procrastination.

Taylor backed her Civic out of the drive, giving a passing wave to Edie, just arriving at the kennel for her morning routine.

When she got to the clinic, she was welcomed by a tall slim blond with a long pony tail, and wearing a name tag that read Danika. Taylor remembered the name from her chat with Darcy yesterday. This was Jonah's ex—girlfriend and the mother of his daughter if gossip was to be believed. She was pretty sure Darcy wouldn't have said anything if she hadn't had her facts right. Danika looked cool and ice—queen elegant in a pale blue two piece uniform.

"Taylor Armstrong for a ten o'clock cleaning," she told

Danika.

Danika took a quick look at her computer screen and said. "Amy will be ready for you in a moment." Then she turned to face Taylor and asked, "Aren't you the one who found Jonah?"

"Yes." said Taylor shortly. It was rapidly becoming her claim to fame in Badger Lake.

"Do you know what's going to happen to Jonah's house now?" Danika asked.

Taylor stared at her for a second before replying. Why would finding a body give her an inside route to the disposition of Jonah's belongings? "I have no idea," she said. "I imagine that's up to his lawyer. If he had one that is."

"Oh, sorry." Danika had obviously reconsidered her question and blushed. "I just thought since you and the RCMP fellow are friends, that you might have heard what was going on." She smiled and gestured to the waiting area. "Have a seat. There's fresh coffee in the machine. I think Amy will be a few minutes longer."

Taylor passed on the coffee. She flicked through the magazines on the table but didn't see anything that caught her fancy. A woman on the chair across the table from her was trying to hold one squirming child while another was trying to rearrange the chairs. The held one was becoming audible in her fight for freedom and the woman gave Taylor an apologetic smile.

On the other end of the line of chairs sat a upright woman with a formidable bosom and steel gray hair. She wore a crisp white blouse under a navy pant suit and no—nonsense shoes that screamed competence and organization. She frowned at the family group until she became aware that Taylor was looking at her. Then she pasted a smile on her face and gave a shrug. Agnes Walker, head of the UCW and town's moral compass.

Seeing her reminded Taylor of the bake sale she had promised to work for. Was it tomorrow? Other things had pushed it to the back of her mind. Thank heavens she had volunteered to be the cash taker, not a donor of baking.

"All ready for tomorrow, Taylor?" Agnes Walker of course knew everyone's role and what would be expected of them.

"Yes," she replied. "Do you have a float for the cash

drawer or should I bring one?"

"Oh we have a float. Everything is taken care of. You merely have to show up."

Taylor wasn't sure whether to take that as a dig as to the sparseness of her contribution, but didn't have time to dwell on it as Amy hailed her for her cleaning.

An hour later and a few dollars poorer, Taylor walked out in the sunlight that somehow seemed a little brighter with her semi-annual ordeal over. Her teeth were cleaned and polished and the dentist had seen no sign of any problems in his brief inspection. The world was now a happier place.

As she drove past the Co-op grocery store, she decided she might as well stop now to pick up a few things for to-night's dinner. The lasagna was lazy—man style, frozen, but she wanted to make a nice salad to go with it. While there, she also picked up some microwave popcorn and soft drinks.

She might as well finish her shopping while she was out so the next stop was the movie rental store. It doubled as a corner store and ice cream shop, open past the regular gro-cery store hours. The choices of movies weren't great. Movie rentals were becoming a thing of the past with all the offer-ings on Netflix or other programs. She finally selected a comedy and a thriller. The men would likely prefer the latter, but maybe they'd have time to sneak in the second movie too. One more stop at the liquor store and she was ready.

Chapter
Seven

As Taylor pulled into her driveway, she noticed a tall, slim woman in jeans and a white shirt with rolled—up sleeves standing in the gravel drive in front of Edie's boarding kennel. Her dark hair was piled on top of her head in a messy bun. The woman was looking around with a puzzled air. She started as Taylor shut her car door, then swung around towards her.

"Are you the owner of the kennel?"

"No", said Taylor, her arms full of her shopping. "But a friend of mine is. I help her out sometimes, so I can help you, or if you'd rather, I can give her a call. Actually her phone number is on the door." Taylor liked helping out at the kennel. After all, it had originally belonged to Aunt Grace along with the house Taylor now lived in. But at the moment she only wanted to rid herself of her shopping burden and get her dinner plans underway.

She set her bags on the hood of the car and rubbed her wrist where the handles had rubbed uncomfortably into her skin. "Is it a dog or a cat you want to board?"

"Neither," the woman said. "I actually don't want to board anything."

Taylor stopped herself from saying "Well what else would you want at a boarding kennel?" Instead she smiled and said, "Well, how can I help you then?"

"I'm sorry," said the woman, putting out her hand. "I should have introduced myself. "I'm Anna Turnbull." She looked expectantly at Taylor as though she should recognize her. "Sorry" she said again. "Of course you don't know who I am. That's my married name. "She took a breath and began again. "I'm Jonah's sister."

"Oh" said Taylor. "You must be here to check on Jonah's dog. Were you planning to take him with you? The police are done with him now so I can get him ready for you."

"No you don't understand. I'm not here to pick up the dog. I couldn't keep him anyway. My son is allergic. No, I just wanted to talk to the woman who found Jonah, so if you could call her for me? They told me the dog came to the kennel and led her to Jonah."

Taylor sighed. This wasn't going to go away easily. "You'd better come in," she said, picking up her shopping. "It wasn't Edie who found Jonah. It was me."

She led Anna into her house, still cool for a summer day and motioned her into the living room. "I'll just put these away and be right with you. I'll put the kettle on."

Instead of following Taylor's suggestion, Anna followed her into the kitchen and sat down on the nearest chair at the kitchen table.

"I'm sorry about your loss," Taylor began tentatively.

"Oh, don't be.' said Anna. "Jonah and I weren't close. Even when we were kids we didn't get along that well. I just wondered how well you knew him."

"Me!" said Taylor flicking the burner under the kettle and turning to face her visitor. "I didn't know him at all."

"But I thought..." began Anna. "You did find him though?"

"Yes."

"So how did you come to find him if you weren't friends?"

Taylor ignored the quotation marks around the word friends and explained simply. "Jonah's dog came, it's the nearest house from where he was found, and sat in front of the boarding kennel howling until I came out to see what was wrong. Then he kept running a few steps and looking back at me as though he wanted me to follow him. I did. He led me to Jonah."

Taylor wished the kettle would boil. Better still she wished she'd offered a cold drink so her visitor would drink and leave. She wasn't unsympathetic to a woman's loss of her brother. After all her own brother Greg's death was still a pain that twisted inside her. But this woman didn't appear to be in the throes of grief and she was beginning to get tired of telling her "how I found Jonah" story.

"Was he...was he still alive when you found him? Did he say anything?" Anna leaned over the table holding Taylor's gaze with an unseemly intensity.

"No to both questions. It was obvious he was dead and I checked for a pulse to be sure but no, he was definitely dead."

Anne sighed, then stood up and reached for her purse.

"The kettle is boiling. I was going to make tea." Taylor had her hand on the now whistling kettle.

"No thanks. I can't stay. If you're sure Jonah didn't have any last words..." She seemed reluctant to believe Taylor which rankled, turning her voice a few shades cooler as she said. "I'm sure. Now what would you like us to do with Jonah's dog? As his sister I imagine you're his next of kin?"

Anne gave a short laugh. "Oh no. I'm not next of kin. That would be our father. He's still alive—well, sort of, in that place at the end of town. But he's in no position to make a decision, so the dog is all yours."

She headed for the door, but stopped with her hand on the knob to look behind her and say. "If you do remember anything Jonah said, I'm staying at the Starlight Motel."

"Well," Taylor said towards the back of her retreating visitor. "Curious and curiouser. I wonder what she expected Jonah's dying words to be. Directions to the hidden family treasure? Deathbed confession?"

No time to think about it now. Taylor had to get her house tidied and the salad things washed and prepped for tonight's dinner. She did give a fleeting thought as to whether or not she should tell Andrew about the visit. *I'll think about that later. He'll be sure to say I'm interfering, and besides, it couldn't have anything to do with Jonah's death.* Taylor thought back to what she'd heard about the family dynamics and wasn't surprised that the children both turned out a little different.

Chapter Eight

Taylor put away her groceries and washed the salad greens. She was glad she'd settled on a lasagna dinner. Cooking had never been Taylor's strong suit and she always preferred to spend her time visiting with her company instead of obsessing over complicated recipes. She had a store-bought apple pie for dessert that could be warmed in the oven and some of Edie's cookies for later. No fancy snack foods either. They would watch the movie nibbling on good old chips and dip.

Sometimes, but not often, Taylor considered taking a cooking course. She knew Darcy could cook streets around her and when she was invited over after the renos, the offerings would definitely not be frozen dinners. When Taylor and Greg were growing up in Aunt Grace's care, they learned a good many things about life but not a lot about cooking. It was time she remedied that hole in her education. Haphazard meals might suit her now, but who knew what lay in her future? She shook her head. *Taylor, what are you thinking?* Darcy's off the cuff comment seemed to have taken up residence in the back of her mind.

She rummaged through her music CDs then opted instead to dock her I-pod and selected an easy-listening play list. She didn't like music blaring in the background but it was nice to have something soft and nonintrusive to cover occasional silences, not that conversational lapses were much of a problem when she and Darcy got together.

Darcy and Dan arrived right on time and they were nearly through a first glass of wine, seated comfortably around the kitchen table, before Andrew appeared on the doorstep.

"Sorry if I'm running late, but I got sidetracked by a visitor." He grinned and held out a handled bag. "I come bearing gifts, though." Taylor thanked him and set the bottle of wine on the kitchen counter.

Andrew didn't look as though he was about to explain further, but Taylor's curiosity bug twitched and she asked, "Jonah's sister?" Too late she remembered she hadn't decided yet whether to tell Andrew about the visit which might make her look as though she were about to get involved in his murder.

Andrew sat down with sigh. "Now why did I think for one moment that we would get through the night without you quizzing me about Jonah?" He frowned at her and followed with "And how do you know about Jonah's sister? Has Edie been giving you the low—down or did you used to know her?"

"Sorry. I wasn't intending to talk about Jonah at all tonight. It just popped into my mind because she was here a little while ago."

"She didn't tell me that. What did she want?"

Now it was Taylor's turn to sigh. She hoped the pleasant evening she had planned wasn't about to go down the tube.

She poured Andrew a glass of wine—he stopped her at the halfway mark as he was driving— and opened the oven door to check the lasagna to give her time to consider her answer. *Oh well, in for a penny, in for a pound.*

"I'm not sure what she wanted. When I got back from shopping she was standing in front of the kennel. When she told me who she was, I assumed she was there to claim Monty. But she said she wasn't interested in the dog. What's going to happen to Monty? Do you know yet? Should we be looking for a home for him? I'd hate to turn him over to the pound, but I can't take another pet and I don't think Edie..."

Andrew cleared his throat. "Taylor. Can you get back to Jonah's sister?"

"Oh. Sorry. Well, I invited her in but she only stayed a few minutes. She seemed interested in how I knew Jonah. She assumed we were 'friends'." Taylor made air quotes for the word. "When I told her I didn't know him, I just found him, she didn't look as though she believed me. Then she asked if he said anything before he died. I told her he was already dead when I got there."

"What did she think he might have said to you?"

"I don't know. I don't think she was looking for 'tell my sister I love her' or 'there'll always be Paris' She actually told me she wasn't going to miss Jonah, that they never got along, even as kids."

"And that's all?"

Taylor considered for a moment. "Yes, that's all. Except for a reference to their father. She didn't sound as though she was going to be making bedside visits to him either. What did she want from you?"

"Taylor, it pains me to say this but it's none of your business. Stay out of this." He softened the order with a smile and reached for her hand. Taylor allowed hers to rest in his for a moment and then said, "What about the house? Who does it belong to now? Did Jonah have a will? Who's next of kin—his sister? His father?" Then she remembered Danika. She looked at Darcy but Darcy had never said the story was a secret. Everyone in town knew, apparently. "Or his daughter?"

"Taylor, haven't you been listening? Stay out of this. Besides, no one is about to inherit the house, because it doesn't belong to Jonah."

"It doesn't?"

Andrew groaned. "I'll tell you this much and then you have to promise to stop asking questions. The house still belongs to Jonah's father. When he started to go downhill a few years ago, Home Care managed to get in touch with Jonah. That's when he came back to Badger Lake. He got a power of attorney, put the old man in the care home and moved into the house. But legally, the house doesn't belong to Jonah. He just had care of it." Andrew tilted his chair back on its rear legs and took a large gulp of wine. "Now, that's all I'm going to say on the matter of Jonah. Let's change the subject. Dan, did you get to try that new boat motor out yet, or have the renos been taking all your time?"

Taylor decided there was no sense in pursuing her questions. Andrew was right. It didn't have anything to do with her. Except she was the one who found the body and she was the one Jonah's sister sought out. She distracted herself by checking the oven and announcing "Dinner's ready!"

Dinner passed with conversation studiously avoiding all references to murder. Dan and Andrew were busy swapping boating and fishing stories and Darcy and Taylor were deep into decorating projects.

"I've decided it's high time I finally began to fix up this place," Taylor's gaze swept over the kitchen—diner with its high, old—fashioned cupboards, worn counter top and 70s flooring. "I made a list of changes when I came back last year, but somehow time has just slipped away and I haven't done a thing." Her expression darkened for a moment. "Except for outside of course." Last year Taylor had been in a hurry to remove the old well from the back yard, a reminder of a portion of her life she didn't want to re—live. That led to fixing up the rest of the yard as well, but the renos had stopped there.

"What do you think?" she asked Darcy. "Should I start with something small—like the bathroom? That would be my first choice."

"I'm the wrong one to ask for advice there. You know me—all or nothing. That's why our entire house is a shambles now: kitchen gutted, bathroom only half functional, and bedroom furniture in the basement. Why piddle away at one room at a time? Go for broke."

"I don't have confidence in my own decorating abilities. I'm afraid of how it might turn out."

"Why not get some help? Maggie Trent, the realtor, is good at doing up houses. She did a fantastic job on the old Sandowski house before they sold it. And the house she lives in now...it's a showpiece."

Maggie Trent had recently bought the real estate company from Jack Vandenberg, who had sold up and disappeared from town after a spot of trouble last year which ended in a nervous breakdown for Jack.

"Any time I mention fixing up to a realtor I get offers to buy, not offers to decorate. And besides, would Maggie be willing to help?" She considered a moment. "You know, it wouldn't hurt to ask. If she had the time and the inclination, she'd be cheaper than a full-time decorator."

"Last I heard, the real estate market in Badger Lake wasn't that great. Look at the For Sale signs in the north end that have been there for months. I bet she has time on her hands and wouldn't mind picking up a few bucks."

"It's worth a try. Next time I see her, I'll sound her out. If it's a casual meeting, then she can change the subject if she's not interested. Thanks, Darcy. That could be a great idea. That way, I might have the nerve to tackle more than just one room at a time."

Taylor got up and started clearing the dishes, piling them in the sink. "I'll leave the dishes soaking. I'll do them later."

"Nonsense. it will only take a few minutes."

"That's one thing on my list of kitchen changes. I always used to think a dishwasher was silly for one person, but I've changed my mind. Instead of leaving the odd dish in the sink waiting for enough to wash, I could hide my slovenly ways by stashing them in the dishwasher till I had a load."

"There! You're already starting to plan. Good start."

"My problem is visualizing. You know those TV shows where they buy old houses and fix them up. They look at a house and can picture what it would like removing a wall, changing a window. I can't see that, unless someone draws me a diagram."

"Then get someone to draw you a diagram, silly. Is that what you want to do—remove a wall here and there? If you took out that wall—she motioned to the one by the table where Andrew and Dan sat—you could get a nice flow into the living room."

Taylor wrinkled her nose. "I know open concept is the big thing now, but I don't know if I want to make such a big change."

Darcy laughed. "Cold feet already, and you haven't even talked to anyone. That's what plans are for. Get Maggie, or someone, to draw up a design and we'll look over it together if you like. Then you can figure out if you like it before knocking down pieces of structure."

Taylor wiped the last of the plates and set it in the cupboard above her, closing the door a second time when it failed to clasp the first. "You're right. It's time to make changes. The cupboards don't close properly, there's a draft in the bedroom from a loose window, everything is outdated and I'll call Maggie this week."

"That's my girl!"

The two men looked up at the exclamation which fell into a gap in their conversation.

"What's up?"

"Taylor is finally going to start re—doing the house. She's

going to talk to Maggie to see if she'll help with decorating."
Andrew looked around. "Oh, I don't know. I kind of like it
the way it is."

Taylor frowned into space. "You do? Maybe I should..."

"Kind of falling apart," Andrew finished. "Just kidding. I
think you're right. It needs a face-lift. But don't ask me for
advice. I thought the Sphinx was fine the way it was."

"Now I need to find a handyman. With Jonah gone..."
Darn. She broken the unspoken rule of the night—no more
references to Jonah.

Oh well. Might as well get on with it. She turned to Andrew and said accusingly. "I thought you were going to come
over and pick up Monty."

"I did."

"I never saw you."

"You were out." Taylor wondered if he had arranged that
deliberately.

"And?" she prompted.

He set down his glass and grinned. "I took Monty for a
drive and parked on Main Street for a while."

"And did he bark at anyone?"

"Yes." He paused as though for effect.

Taylor glared at him. "He barked at a total of seven people. One of them was Mrs. Napier who merely rolled past the
truck with her wheelchair. Sorry."

"No. I'm sorry I sent you off on a wild goose chase."

"As I said before, it wasn't the craziest idea you ever had.
It was worth a try. Of course a barking dog wouldn't impress
a judge in court, but if he really lunged at someone, it could
have given me a direction."

Andrew picked up his glass again but didn't have time to
do more than lift it to his mouth. His cell rang and he stood
up, turning his back to them and exiting to the living room as
he answered.

A moment later he was back. "Sorry, we'll have to do the
movie another night."

"What happened?" Taylor was glad her voice wasn't the
only one raising the question.

Andrew hesitated. "A caller just reported someone snooping around Jonah's house." He grabbed his jacket and pock-
eted his cell, grabbing his keys. "Talk to you tomorrow."

Chapter Nine

The three sat in silence. All the energy in the room seemed to have departed with Andrew.

It was Darcy who spoke first. "I wonder if Danika knows Jonah didn't own the house."

"Would she care?"

"Well, if her daughter is Jonah's she could make a case for ownership. If the house belonged to Jonah.... and if he didn't leave a will."

"That's a lot of 'ifs,'" said Dan.

"Besides," said Taylor. "Didn't you tell me she wasn't even taking support from him? Sounds like an independent woman to me."

"Yes, that was strange."

"How so?"

"I remember she went after him for support when Franny was born. I think she wanted him to marry her. Of course he wasn't having any of that. I don't think Jonah is the marrying kind. But then she gave up."

"She must have decided he was the proverbial stone you couldn't get money out of."

"Mmm. Maybe. "

"Okay, Darcy, give. What do you know that we don't?"

"Not much, really. But I know for a fact that Jonah is listed as father on the birth certificate."

"How do you know that?"

"Because I saw it. When Jonah came back to Badger

Lake, Danika started after Jonah for support again. She was-
n't working at the dental clinic then. She worked with me—at
the insurance office. And she copied the certificate on the
office copier. She must have had it crooked or something
first go and she tore it up and threw that copy in the trash."
Darcy reddened a little as she looked up at the other two.
"Okay, I'm a snoop. I'm not proud of it. but later I dug the
pieces out of the trash to look."

"Ah—ha!" cried Taylor.

"What?'" Darcy looked alarmed at the vehemence of Taylor's exclamation.

"Everyone is always telling me I'm too curious for my
own good and should put a lid on my snooping. And there
you are." She sat back with a satisfied smirk. "I'm just glad
I'm not the only one."

"I think I'm getting sorry I told you," said Darcy.

"Oh sorry Darcy. I wasn't criticizing you." Taylor grinned.
"More like welcoming you into the group."

Dan gave them an exasperated look.

Darcy glared at him. "Don't try to make this into a 'wom-
en are always poking their noses into everyone's business,
what can you do about them' thing. You're the one who told
me next day you saw Jonah and Danika in the lawyer's office
together."

"I did?"

"Yes. Don't you remember?"

"If you say so." Dan got up to open a beer and offered
wine to Taylor. She shook her head.

Darcy rolled her eyes at his back and took a swig of juice.

"Anyhow, it looked to me as though they were settling on
something together about Franny. Then all of a sudden she
appeared to drop it. I overheard her saying to someone she
intended to raise her daughter with no help from anyone and
that included her father."

"Everyone can change their minds. Maybe she decided it
was better for Franny to keep him out of her life."

"Maybe." Darcy didn't sound convinced.

"So," broke in Dan, ending the paternity conversation
once and for all. "Are we going to watch a movie? I doubt if
Andrew is going to be back tonight."

Taylor led them into the living room and shooed Denver

from the couch. He gave her a dirty look and stalked off towards the stairs. Taylor knew he'd be back once they brought out the snacks. Tristan never even tried to hide his plan to panhandle. He stretched out on the floor in front of the couch, darting his eyes back and forth to see who would be the easiest mark.

Taylor slid the DVD into the slot and switched the TV to video. "Sorry Dan, but you're outvoted. It's the chic—flick, not the car—chase one."

Dan groaned good-naturedly and leaned back in his seat, lowering his hand to Tristan whose tail began to beat a happy tattoo on the carpet. "Don't give him enough to make him sick," she cautioned. "Cream cheese doesn't always agree with him."

Her mind flicked to Andrew's call-out. She wondered who had tried to break in to Jonah's house and why. She knew there were always people who scanned obituary pages looking for targets, but that wasn't a small town thing. Here everyone knew all the births and deaths before the papers came out.

Someone wanted something of Jonah's. She wondered if it were the same person who had killed him.

Chapter
Ten

Taylor slept in the next morning. Or at least as much as a person who lives with a dog and a cat can sleep in. It was Denver who woke her up, pawing at her hair. She flicked a hand up to shoo him away and wiggled her tongue around in her dry mouth. *Shouldn't have had that second glass of wine.*

Reluctantly, she pulled herself out of bed. She shooed Tristan out to the back yard while she went to the bathroom to perform her morning ablutions. Denver kept vigil outside the door, just to be sure his breakfast wouldn't be forgotten.

Animals fed and a second cup of coffee poured, Taylor felt much better. She was glad they had washed the dinner dishes last night. She didn't feel like facing congealing food this morning, but all that lay in the sink were the glasses, a couple of snack plates and an empty popcorn bowl.

She wondered about the break—in at Jonah's and if they actually got into the house and if the burglar had been caught. What could they be looking for? She remembered his sister's questions about the house and Danika's interest in her finding the body. Strange—no one had liked Jonah apparently, but everyone was concerned about his death. And about her role in discovering his body.

She put away the milk and glanced at the memo in the fridge magnet. *Oh great. Today is the Bake Sale.* She was thankful her role was only to take the cash at the end table. She could leave the baking to her betters, like Edie, whose cinnamon buns would be one of the star offerings.

She spent an hour playing with her list of renos, trying to decide which ones were realistic, and which were pie in the sky. She sighed. The only way to find out would be to phone Jimmy and ask him to come by for appraisal and estimate. If she did it one room at a time, maybe he'd be able to fit her in. She knew he didn't take on major projects, but surely a bathroom update, or new kitchen cabinets? She gave him a call and he promised to come over Monday morning to take a look.

"Hey Tristan. Maybe he'll bring Felix and you can have a play date." Felix was Jimmy's boxer who went everywhere with him. Taylor thought it a strange name for a dog, but he had come to Jimmy with that name. Felix had once belonged to Tara Leigh, an old friend of Greg's who had died last year in a series of events that had led Taylor into a fight for her life.

Tristan bounded up, tail quivering and head cocked to the side in anticipation. He recognized the tone of voice that usually meant something was coming to relieve the boredom.

"Sorry old fellow. I didn't mean today." But Tristan was already across the room, standing by the hook that held his leash.

"Okay, okay. I could do with some fresh air."

As she opened the front door she nearly ran into a visitor standing on her step with a hand raised as though about to knock. Anna, Jonah's sister lowered her hand.

"Oh you're going out," she said. "Sorry, I'll come back another time."

"No, that's all right. We were only going for a walk. It can wait." She opened the door wider and re-entered, pulling a seriously annoyed Jack Russell inside after her. "Later," she said to Tristan. "Good boy." She unsnapped his leash.

Anna followed her in. Her manner today was a far cry from her last visit. She was actually smiling.

Taylor led her into the kitchen. "Coffee?" she asked. There were still a couple of small cups worth left in the carafe, not yet stale. It would do.

Tristan had followed them into the kitchen, sniffed at Anna and apparently decided she wasn't worth his interest. He thumped into his dog bed in the corner and turned his back on them in a sulk, a stunt more feline than canine in nature. "Yes, thanks," said Anna. Taylor poured the coffee and set out cream and sugar which Anna declined. "I came to apologize," she said. "I was rather rude yesterday."

"No problem," Taylor replied and then winced at her use of a phrase which had always annoyed her when others used it. "I realize you were still in shock over Jonah's death."

"Not exactly in shock. Like I said Jonah and I weren't close. Most of the time I couldn't stand him. It started with the usual sibling problems, I guess, but it didn't go away when we got older."

She sipped her coffee and reached for the sugar. "I think I'll sweeten it after all."

Uh—oh thought Taylor. It's more stewed than I thought. She took a sip of her own and made a face. "Old," she said, and reached for Anna's cup. "Let me throw it out and make fresh."

Anna shook her head. "No thanks. I didn't really want coffee anyhow, I just took it to be sociable." She set the cup aside and went on. "Did Jonah have anything on him when you found him?"

"Like what?"

"Like a notebook, or a letter—maybe a letter in an old envelope? Anything beside him or in his pocket?"

"Anna, I didn't exactly search him when I found him. Like I said, he was definitely dead. I felt for a pulse and backed off immediately and called for help. I wasn't about to rifle his pockets." Surely Jonah hadn't been blackmailing his own sister!

She decided to put it into a question. After all, Anna owed her an explanation.

"He wasn't blackmailing you too, was he?"

Anna looked startled. "No. Blackmailing?" Then she smiled again, but it wasn't the pleasant one she had pasted on her face earlier. "I'm not surprised though. Jonah would do anything for a buck."

"So what were you expecting him to have on him that I might have found?"

Anna sat back in her chair and hugged herself, lifting her shoulders as though to protect herself from some unseen onslaught.

"Jonah had something I wanted," she said. "Something he promised me and didn't deliver."

"What? A will? A cheque? A letter?"

"I might as well tell you," she said. "It doesn't matter who knows." She took a breath and went on. "I wanted to find out who my real father was."

"You were adopted?"

"No. But I don't think the man in the Care Home is my father. I never did." She stopped briefly as though to collect her thoughts.

"I always thought I was different from them—from Jonah and Dad, that is. I know I was born less than nine months after they were married. I guess that doesn't mean anything. He could still be my father. It was mostly a feeling I had. And then it was the way Mom reacted when I began to ask questions. I kept badgering her about my real father and instead of insisting Dad was my real father, she would get evasive and just tell me not to ask questions I might not like the answer to. That was what convinced me Dad wasn't my real Dad." She unthinkingly reached for the coffee cup and took another sip before realizing what she was drinking. She made a face and set it back. Taylor considered making that fresh pot but was afraid to move and dry up the line of narrative.

"I wasn't here when Mom died. I had pretty much put my family back into a past life by then. But I did come back for a while when she got really sick. I didn't stay long, Dad and Jonah were both there. I didn't want to be around them. I stayed long enough to say my goodbyes, because we knew she was going to die soon. I asked her again about my father and she made some cryptic comment about my never knowing while she had breath in her body. I took that to mean I'd find out sometime. After she was gone, I asked Jonah if she had left me anything, a letter or document. He said no but since he always lied to me, I didn't know whether to believe him or not. He was her executor—Jonah was always Mom's favourite, no matter what he did. She really had nothing to leave anyhow. I flew back for the funeral and only stayed till she was in the ground. I went back home to get on with my life.

"Then out of the blue, I heard from Jonah. He asked me if I had been expecting a letter from Mom after she died. I got really excited then and asked him what he found. Then he did what Jonah always did—tried to get what he could out of it. He told me if I sent him five hundred dollars, he'd see I got the letter. I sent him the money but he never answered. That was a couple of weeks ago. so when I heard he'd died, I thought maybe he still had it."

"You were the one," said Taylor.

"The one what?"

"The one who was hanging around Jonah's house."

"Technically not Jonah's house," she said. "Dad's house I think. And I had every right to be there. I still had my key. I found it in an old cigar box of junk I had in the back of my closet and brought it along just in case. I used a key to get in and looked everywhere but I couldn't find anything. Then I thought I heard someone outside and disappeared out the back way before I got caught."

"Caught? But if you had every right to be there..."

Anna sighed. "Caught was maybe the wrong term to use, but I didn't want to answer questions about what I was doing there. With Jonah murdered, I thought it might look bad."

"But now you've told me. Don't you think you should tell the police too? If anyone has access to Jonah's papers, they will." Taylor didn't add that she knew Anna had already made one visit to the police station.

"I already talked to the police."

"But did you tell them all this? Maybe they have what you're looking for."

"You're right. I have a right to know what they have." she stood and said, "Thanks for the coffee," then grinned and added, "Well maybe not. You know, it wouldn't surprise me if Jonah had nothing. He just saw my paternity questions as a way to make a few dollars. Maybe that miserable old sod in the hospital really is my father and everything else was my imagination."

"Have you ever tried to ask him?"

"Dad? He can't tell the truth any more than Jonah could. Besides, from what I hear, he's only half there most of the time anyhow. Still—maybe you're right. Maybe now would be the time to ask him. Without having all his wits about him, he might let something slip. If there is anything to let slip."

She headed for the door, not waiting for Taylor to see her out. Tristan jumped up from his bed and stared unblinkingly at Taylor.

"All right, all right," she said. "Back to our original plan." She reached for his leash, wondering if Anna had been the prowler someone had reported or if there had been someone else. Anna said she'd heard a car, but if it had been Andrew, he would have checked the back lane and probably run into her. Maybe the prowler came later. She should have asked Anna what time she was there.

Hopefully Anna would talk to Andrew again, this time a little more honestly. but truth—telling didn't seem to run in the Whitcomb family.

The sky was nearly cloudless and the morning sun just warm enough to be pleasant, not hot enough to make walking a chore. Tristan pulled right as they entered the back lane. His favourite walk was the one that led past the cemetery but from there the road led to the nuisance grounds, and Taylor would give that route a pass for the foreseeable future. Tristan grumbled dog—fashion but gave up and trotted quickly alongside Taylor, willing to find adventure in any direction.

They headed south, in the area of the lake, but made a right turn towards the outskirts of town. The streets here held a mixture of architecture, some old brick houses standing like stern matrons on large gardened lots, interspersed with new builds, some merely replacements on old lots and one or two so new that the sod lines were still visible in the lawns.

It was at one of the old matrons that Tristan suddenly heeded the call and he pulled over to a pristine lawn to begin his nature dance. "Oh Tristan, couldn't you wait for the back lane?" Taylor glanced up and saw that this particular house belonged to, of course, Agnes Walker. And a face showed through the curtains, taking in the scene on her front lawn. "I'm picking up. I'm picking up," Taylor murmured, preparing her doggie—bag for a scoop. The face remained at the curtains until dog, owner and bag had left the edge of the lawn. "Why that house Tristan? Couldn't you have gone when I gave you a chance by the vacant lot? Or waited till we hit the back road?" She tied a knot in the baggie and they went on, Tristan happily ready to concentrate on more important things.

They took a turn back towards the lake down a street that had been occupied since Badger Lake's beginnings and the houses looked the same as they must have then. No new builds on this street. As they passed a two storey house with white siding and green, freshly painted shutters, she saw a vehicle she recognized. The blue truck left no doubt as to its ownership. The Handyman Can was emblazoned across the side door as well as across the back window of the cab. *I guess the police would tow it home after forensics was done with it. And Andrew took Monty on his foray downtown.* She slowed until Tristan looked up inquiringly. *I don't see any sign of a break-in.* But then Andrew hadn't described it as a break-in only as someone prowling the yard. Maybe they never got inside. Maybe that was Anna's visit, or was there a second prowler. Then she noticed a second marked vehicle parked on the street just past the drive. On the ground beside it, not yet dug in, was a sign that read For Sale. *How could they be selling the house so soon? Especially if Jonah didn't really own it.*

She realized it could be a good time to talk to Maggie Trent and pick her brain about redecorating ideas. Maybe she'd agree to be a consultant, for a fee of course, but hopefully not a big fee. Taylor couldn't afford a real interior decorator.

She walked up the drive, tugging at a puzzled Tristan who pulled back at first then gave in, probably hoping he might meet a new friend with treats.

There was no other vehicle in front. Maggie was likely taking pictures or staging the house for a sale. She wouldn't be showing anyone around yet. The sign wasn't even up. There didn't appear to be a doorbell so she tapped gently on the door and called out softly, just in case. She didn't want to interrupt a potential sale. No answer so she turned the door handle. Locked. Maybe Maggie was around the back. Taylor skirted the house and looped Tristan's leash over a post on the railing. She dropped her baggie beside him. She repeated her actions at this door, tapping first and then trying the handle. Maggie obviously didn't want to be interrupted. Taylor stood for a moment, biting her lower lip. She should just leave, but she didn't want to miss a golden opportunity to get Maggie alone.

The curtains at the large living room window were tightly closed as were the dining room blinds. Taylor shaded her eyes from the glare on the small, single pane window in the outer door, peering inside. She couldn't see Maggie. She noticed the contents of a desk in the living room that appeared to have been strewn around. Was that why Andrew had been called in? There was no sign of a police presence here so maybe the reported break-in was just someone's imagination. In any case, there mustn't have been much to it if Maggie had been allowed to set it up for sale.

Her eyes adjusted and she could see further down the hallway, past the desk. A door, probably a bedroom door, stood slightly ajar. She stiffened at the sight of a moving figure. It was Maggie. Well, not Maggie exactly, as she couldn't see into the room itself. but a reflection of Maggie in the vanity mirror.

She quickly clamped a hand over her mouth to stop any sound from coming out and turned and fled from the step, grabbing Tristan's leash from the post as she ran into the back lane, searching for cover before she could be seen. Could Maggie have heard her?

She crouched behind an SUV that stood behind the back lane dumpster until she was sure no one had followed her from the house. She didn't know who would be more embarrassed, the occupants of the house for being seen, or Taylor, for being caught seeing them. For the brief glimpse of Maggie that Taylor had caught had been a different Maggie to the one she knew. This one was dressed in black, from the tall leather boots and the black fishnets above them, to the bustier. And crowning it all was the black whip she held in her right hand. Taylor hadn't seen the second occupant to identify him, but as she dissolved into a silent heaving burst of laughter, she suddenly recognized the vehicle she was crouched behind. She had had many dealings with him the past year when she inherited the house from Aunt Grace. For the Ford Escape she was hiding behind belonged to Melvin Donovan, the attorney.

Taylor stood slowly and, seeing no one around, left her

compromising crouched position behind the Escape. She walked down the back lane as sedately as she could, tugging Tristan after her.

It wasn't until she reached her driveway that she realized she had forgotten something. The bright blue baggie containing evidence of Tristan's nature call was sitting beside the back door railing.

Well, there goes my plan to use Maggie's expertise as a decorator. Not only would she worry that Maggie would notice the baggie and put two and two together, but she wouldn't be able to stifle her unpredictable bursts of giggles any time the picture she had just seen popped back into her mind.

Chapter Eleven

Taylor tried to busy herself at her computer to chase away the image that seemed etched into her brain. But, with every pause in her work, came a return of the scene and a fresh burst of laughter.

She was happy to hear her doorbell. Something to distract her. It was Edie, with a plate of deliciously smelling cinnamon buns. "I've been at them since about four this morning," said Edie, "Getting ready for the bake sale. I saw you coming back from your walk with Tristan and thought you might be ready for a treat."

Tristan heard the last word and perked up his ears, assuming the word was directed at him.

"Not your cup of tea, Tristan," said Taylor, "But we'll find something for you too." She followed Edie into the kitchen and asked, "Tea or coffee?"

"Oh tea, I think. I've been drinking coffee since dawn." Taylor put the kettle on and took out the mugs. She set out the milk too, as the tea was bound to be too strong for her when it got to Edie strength.

"How did your dinner go last night? Is Darcy having morning sickness?"

"Now how did you know? I didn't think she'd told anyone yet. You always amaze me Edie. Sometimes I think you're part psychic."

"Nothing so exotic. I know Dan's Aunt Phoebe and I gather the family just got the news. She called me last night and she sounded quite excited at the prospect."

"The dinner went fine," Taylor went back to the first question. "That is, until Andrew got a call. Someone apparently tried to break into Jonah's house and he was off. I haven't heard from him since, so I don't know anything more."

Edie seemed to sense that wasn't the whole story, "But? I do sense a 'but' in there, don't I?"

Taylor decided she might as well tell Edie the whole story. "Well, Tristan and I walked down towards the lake this morning and when we passed Jonah's house I saw Maggie's car and thought I'd sound her out..." She went on to tell the rest of the story, but somehow in retrospect it didn't seem as funny when she related the details. Or maybe she was just laughed out. She could tell by the twitch at the corners of Edie's mouth that she found it amusing.

"So, why do you think the house is for sale now if Jonah didn't even own it?"

Edie pondered. "Maybe the Power of Attorney laid out what happened if Jonah died before his father. Or maybe someone else was listed on the document as well. Or maybe..." But she seemed to have run out of maybes.

"Either one of those scenarios would explain Melvin Donovan's presence—outside of the ER... Well, if he drew up the document, he'd be able to set things in motion right away. And if he were also an executor or whatever they call it under the Power of Attorney, he'd also be able to dispose of it. Which means he probably also has Jonah's will."

"If he made a will," said Edie. "He was a young man and still of an age where he possibly never considered his mortality."

"Oh of course. I haven't made a will. I suppose someday I should, but there's lots of time. But there wasn't for Jonah, was there? What do you think everyone is looking for? An attempted break in." She thought back to her visit from Anna. But she would have been looking with time on her hands, no need to scatter things around. Maybe the person she thought she heard was the searcher.

"The desk was all turned out. I wonder if that was done by a burglar or if Maggie and Melvin were looking for something?"

"But what?"

"That's the sixty four thousand dollar question. And, just like last year, everyone seems to think I know the answer."

"Andrew is right, Taylor. Keep out of this—for your own good,"

"I have no intention of getting mixed up in Andrew's investigation. But people keep asking me about it. They seem to think I should know."

"Who?"

"Jonah's sister Anne, for starters. Then Danika."

"That's two people, Taylor; hardly a horde. It's just normal small town curiosity."

"Oh, with all the kerfuffle over Maggie's little—well, whatever you call it, I forgot to tell you I had another visit from Anna."

She went on to describe Anna's quest for paternity proof. "Do you think that puts her on the list of suspects? If Jonah wouldn't tell her what she thought he knew maybe she figured she'd find out if he died."

"That's a little far-fetched for a murder motive. In fact the whole blackmailing thing is a little thin, don't you think? No one in this town seems to have done anything to warrant murder as a cover-up. Jonah knew the worth of his information and how far people would go to cover up their peccadilloes. He only asked for a few dollars here and there. People would only laugh at him as I did, if they didn't care enough to keep secrets, or report him and be damned if he got too greedy. He walked a fine line, but seems to have known his customers and exactly what his limits were."

Taylor sighed. "You're right. Time to forget about Jonah and think about something else. What time are you going to the Bake Sale? Do you want a lift?"

"Thanks. It would save me firing up my old beater. I don't think I've had it out of the garage for months. I should sell it someday, I suppose. I rarely use it."

"Wait a few years," said Taylor with a grin, "and it will qualify as an antique."

When Edie left, Taylor pondered lunch prospects. She wasn't really hungry now after Edie's offering of cinnamon buns, but she didn't want to go to the bake sale on an empty stomach. Edie's buns were bad enough, but then there was

Jessie Ford's lemon slice and Agnes Walker's homemade bread, amongst other goodies she knew would be for sale. She would spend most of the afternoon surrounded by sweet smells. The only way not to cave in to temptation would be to start with a full stomach. Of course she'd have to buy something to bring home. After all, raising money was the point of a bake sale.

She opted for a grilled cheese sandwich with a side of cucumber and red pepper slices. The greasy sandwich would fill her up and the veggies would be an offering to the nutrition gods.

She tidied up after lunch and let Tristan out in the back yard for a quick pee before heading out for the sale. She detoured to the post office on the way to check for mail, before making a U—turn to the back lane to pick up Edie. In this electronic age, most of the paper mail was junk, but you never knew. As she opened the door to the post office, heading for the wall of boxes, she nearly bumped into Andrew, on his way out.

"Oh hi Taylor," he said. "Sorry, can't stop." He was out the door so quickly Taylor barely had time to grunt out a reply. *He looks like a kid caught with his hand in the cookie jar. He had seemed his old self over dinner. Now this. What in the world is wrong with him these days. Or is it me?*

She peered into the main lobby of the building but could see no one there that would inspire Andrew's guilty look. An elderly man who lived a few blocks over and Mrs. Buchanan, matron of the Senior's Home. Maybe something he got in the mail? He had a clutch of letters in his left hand. Bad news? But it wasn't a bad news look he had been wearing, it was a guilty one.

Taylor shook her head. She was going to have to come right out and ask Andrew what was going on if she wanted to know. But did she want to know?

Edie was waiting for her by the back door and they loaded her substantial offerings into the back seat of Taylor's Civic.

Tomorrow she'd worry about Andrew. Today she'd concentrate on the sale.

Chapter
Twelve

The hall was a hive of activity. Tables were set up and covered with cloths. Ladies were setting out their wares on their allotted portions and, overseeing it all with her usual mantle of efficiency and leadership, was Agnes Walker.

Edie made directly for the table where she displayed her cinnamon buns at every sale. There appeared to be an un-written law that stated each participant had their regular spot. No one ever tried to usurp another's location. Not with-out repercussions.

"Can I help set up?" Taylor ventured.

"I think everything is in hand," said Agnes Walker. "All you need to do is get organized at the end of the far table. I'll get you the cash drawer." She marched into the kitchen alcove and picked up a black box which she handed to Tay-lor. "Grab a folding chair from the pile in the corner. If you start to run short of any coins or bills, be sure and let me know in plenty of time so I can send someone to the bank."

Neatly dismissed, Taylor did as she was told. The doors were propped open and a couple of early birds were already beginning a promenade down the right row of tables. Taylor slipped down to the closest area where Nina, the organist from church, was just arriving with a large open box. She was breathless and gave a quick glance in Agnes Walker's direction to see if her tardiness had been noted. It had. With a reciprocated smile and greeting, Taylor began to help her unpack. When they were done, she looked up at the transformed tables, now filled with everything from breads to jams and preserves, jars of pickles and every kind of dainty known to church ladies universally.

It was one of those times that made Taylor glad she had come back to live in Badger Lake. This was small town living at its best. Everyone pitching in to share and help. Taylor's first customer appeared with a jar of dill pickles and two paper plates of oatmeal and raisin cookies. Taylor made change and placed the cookies in a plastic bag which she handed over with a smile. "Thanks, Mrs. Bewcyk. Those cookies look so good. I'm going to have to pick up some myself before they're all gone."

"It's the dill pickles I came for. The cookies were an impulse. Nancy Malitaere is the best pickle maker in town. I should have got two." She frowned for a moment at her pickle jar as though considering a return trip to the table.

Then she brought up the topic Taylor had hoped would stay buried. "I see Jonah's funeral notice is up in the Post Office. It's scheduled for Monday afternoon. I don't imagine there will be a big turnout." Then she looked at Taylor in an almost accusing way. "They said you found the body. I hope this isn't going to be a repeat of last year."

Taylor was saved from having to reply by a plonk of another pickle jar on the table. Kelly appeared behind Mrs. Bewcyk and said with a wink. "Hi Taylor. She's right. Best pickles in town." She passed over a five dollar bill.

Mrs. Bewcyk reluctantly turned away. Obviously she had wanted dibs on whatever gossip Taylor could hand out.

When she was out of earshot Taylor whispered, "Thanks Kelly. I hope that's not an indication of how the afternoon is going to go." she sighed. "And here I was thinking how nice it was to be back living in a small town again."

"It still is." said Kelly. "But sometimes I agree with you. It would be a lot better if people could just learn to mind their own business. And Jonah himself was top of the list there." Her face had clouded over in an uncharacteristic way for the usually sunny Kelly. But, quicksilver like, the smile was back. "I never have time to make my own pickles with four boys in a constant state of motion, and store bought ones are never as good." She took her change from Taylor and said goodbye with a quick wave.

Brenda Prentiss, the minister's wife, had joined Agnes Walker in the tiny kitchen and they soon appeared with a large coffee urn and jugs of sugar and milk for a table set up just outside the kitchen doorway. Brenda gave her a wave and, with a quick look at Agnes whose attention seemed to have settled elsewhere, came over to Taylor. She had a coffee cup in her hand. "I thought you might like a cup," she said. "I just brought black but if you need cream and sugar..."

"No thanks. Black is fine. And thank you."

Brenda reminded Taylor of a 1950s sitcom mom. She always wore a dress or skirt, usually accompanied by high heels. In church, she was the only woman that still wore a hat. Maybe she felt pressure because of her position as minister's wife. But Taylor remembered the last preacher's wife they had before she left Badger Lake. While she always looked presentable at church, Beth's outfit of choice around the house had been jeans and a t-shirt. Today Brenda wore a flower-patterned, knee-length dress with elbow sleeves, a high neck and a slight flare to the skirt. She wore her trademark heels which boosted her five foot nothing height a little. Maybe that was the point.

"It seems to be starting a little slowly," said Taylor. "I haven't been busy yet."

"Oh that will change. No one ever likes to arrive first. They wait till there are lots of others so they can stop for a gossip and coffee."

Brenda stood still, scanning the room as though doing a head count, twisting a jade pendant at her throat. Her fingers clutched it so tightly Taylor feared for the longevity of the chain.

She looked back at Taylor. "When you found Jonah..." She stopped there.

"Yes," said Taylor, drawing out the word in anticipation. She had known from the coffee session at the Northland that Brenda had something on her mind.

"Did he have a black notebook, or a letter, on him?"

"I don't remember seeing one," said Taylor, "but considering the circumstances, I wasn't noticing anything other than Jonah." She couldn't stop from asking the obvious "Why?"

"Oh, it's nothing important." Brenda dropped her hold on

the pendant. "It's just that he was going to do a landscaping job for me in the back garden and I think he had some drawings in it. No problem." She turned on a spiky heel and returned to the company of Agnes Walker who had begun to peer around, looking for her.

Now that is strange. Not that Brenda should be getting work done by Jonah but her whole manner—nervous, hesitant and worried. Yes, worried. that would be the best word to describe it. Why would a minister's wife be worried about a black book carried around by the local handyman? Taylor didn't believe for a moment the story about the landscaping drawings.

She didn't have time to ponder. The arrivals Brenda predicted were beginning to show up and she was soon busy taking cash for the sales.

With all the delicious scents passing under her nose, Taylor was beginning to feel hungry, in spite of her substantial lunch. Maybe she could take a break if a lull came and grab something decadent. She knew the coffee she had just finished would be looking for an outlet, so at some point she'd have to flag down Agnes or Brenda to mind the cash while she went for a bathroom break. But she could hold on a while longer. She glanced at her watch. Only an hour or so to go yet. Maybe she could last.

She looked towards the entrance to see how many newcomers were arriving. A large figure stood in the doorway with the sun behind him, so that Taylor couldn't recognize him. Then the figure moved into the building and Taylor recognized Hank, Kelly's husband. He briefly scanned the tables and made his way to Taylor's cash counter.

"Seen Kelly today?"

"She was here not that long ago," said Taylor. "Bought some pickles."

"She was supposed to meet me for coffee at Nick's at three-thirty." His expression was annoyed, his voice exasperated. Taylor had noted the time a moment ago and it was only a few minutes past three-thirty. Hank's annoyance seemed out of proportion.

"She left here a half hour ago. she's probably at the coffee shop now. Maybe you just missed her."

He nodded and said, "Yes, you're probably right. I know I

worry too much about her, but she's been feeling a little, well off, lately. I like to keep an eye on her." Then he broke into a lopsided grin that gave his formerly grim face instant charm. At that moment Taylor could picture his visage on the cover of a romance novel. No wonder Kelly had been smitten with him. He must have made quite a change from all the boys that had pursued her in school.

She ran over Hank's words after he left. Had Kelly seemed 'off' lately? Not that she had seen, but then you never knew what went on behind closed doors. Hank seemed genuinely worried. Taylor hoped nothing was wrong. She liked Kelly. A thought sprung up. Maybe she was pregnant again. That could cause a jump in the hormones.

She realized she was running short of quarters and waved towards the table where Agnes reigned. It was Brenda who answered the wave and came over. Taylor said, "Sorry but I'm running low on change. Could you get someone to run over for two rolls of quarters? Oh, and maybe a roll of loonies too?"

"I'll go myself," Brenda said brightly. "I'm ready for fresh air." *And probably also a chance to escape Agnes.* Taylor sympathized. Agnes Walker was a woman of good works, full of duty and kind acts. But somehow Taylor always felt wanting under her eye of scrutiny and she imagined others did as well. Every small town needed at least one Agnes Walker to make sure things got done. But that didn't make them the most sought after company.

Taylor looked up to lock glances with Maggie Trent. She looked down quickly and began counting her change as an excuse to avoid Maggie's stare. Because she thought she read accusation in Maggie's expression. *Just guilt, Taylor, at being caught snooping.* But she hadn't been caught. There must be dozens of people in town who used those same bright blue doggie-doo bags. It could have been left behind by anyone, and at any time. When she looked up again Maggie had moved down the line. She steeled herself for the coming conversation, because Maggie held a tray of cinnamon buns in her hand so she intended buying.

A few customers went through her line to take her mind off Maggie. Then suddenly, she was there. "I love Edie's buns," she said. "I'm sure offering them has helped me make a sale or two." Taylor relaxed. Thank heavens Maggie was going to keep the conversation on the bake sale.

"They're my favourite too," agreed Taylor.

Maggie paid for her purchase and looked behind her at the nonexistent lineup before saying, "When you found Jonah..."

Taylor groaned. Here it came again.

"Did he have anything in his hands? Or on the truck seat?'

"Like what?"

She leaned over and lowered her voice to a near whisper. "A black notebook." She seemed to search for a viable explanation. "It's just that I had been talking to him about renovations on the old Sandowski place and he had some plans and estimates for me. I thought the information could help getting someone new to do the work."

"No," said Taylor. "I didn't see any notebook. but then I wasn't really up to noticing anything except Jonah at the time."

"Of course." Maggie straightened and smiled. "Not important. I'll make do."

Taylor was searching under her table for more bags when she heard a clunk on the top. "Two rolls of quarters and one of loonies as requested, Ma'am." She looked up at Andrew.

"How did you? I gave the money to Brenda."

"I met her coming out of the bank and she said you needed change pronto. Also that she had an errand to run so could I please bring it to you."

"Thanks, Andrew. Strange. I wonder what sort of errand she so suddenly thought of?"

Andrew gave an exasperated sigh. "Taylor, everything isn't a puzzle or a mystery you have to solve. Maybe she just remembered she was out of butter."

"Or maybe she saw an opportunity to escape Agnes for a while."

"There you go. Perfectly rational explanation. See you later." She watched him leave, silhouetted in the doorway for a moment before he stepped outside. She concluded he was acting normal again, except for his exasperation at her curiosity. But then that was normal too. She had probably been imagining his changes in demeanour, she decided. He was busy after all and this murder must be preying on his mind. That probably explained his changes in mood. She decided not to worry about it anymore. If he had something to tell her, he would.

Traffic began to slow down as people slipped off to their homes to begin dinner preparations or check on families. In no time at all, Agnes closed the big main door behind the last customer and the bakers began to gather the scant remains of their offerings.

Taylor emptied her cashbox and began to count. When she went to hand her takings to Agnes she realized Brenda never had come back.

Chapter Thirteen

Taylor, exiting the lineup of those paying homage to Agnes with comments about how well the sale had gone, collected Edie and was quite happy to step outside into the sunshine. Edie had no cinnamon buns left, as expected—they were always a hot item—but had replaced them with a container of blueberry muffins.

Taylor had managed to abstain from nibbling while the sale went on but happily clutched a package of the oatmeal raisin cookies as well as a tray of brown sugar fudge.

As they neared home, Edie said, "Want to stop in at my place for coffee? Maybe we can do some sampling?"

"Love to. I'll just run in for a minute to let Tristan out." She pulled into her own drive and left the car running with the AC on.

"Don't worry about leaving the car on," said Edie, opening her door. "I'll check on Monty while you're gone." She headed next door to the Boarding Kennel. Each dog had a large run with a set off area for nature calls, so Monty at least wouldn't be crossing his legs like Tristan. But he was the only dog in the kennel now, so would be lonely.

A few minutes later Taylor was back behind the wheel, joining Edie who had already returned. "Tristan wasn't too happy with me," Taylor said. "Thank heavens for the aloofness of cats. I don't think Denver even noticed I was gone. How is Monty doing?"

"He at least wags his tail now when I come in. And on this morning's walk, he forgot himself for a moment and tried to chase a squirrel, so I think he's on the mend. It will take time, though. He went everywhere with Jonah. What he really needs is a good home." Taylor saw a picture of Andrew flash quickly across her view but pushed the thought away. Andrew seemed in no hurry to get a new dog. Still—it was a thought. If she brought it into conversation casually, maybe he'd pick up on it. After this case was solved, of course. It appeared no one else was going to claim the dog. Besides, who was going to pay Edie the kennel fees she was due? Edie couldn't board him forever, and she already had one dog. So did Taylor.

Edie checked on Jasper who had been guarding his back yard with due diligence and brought him in for treats and attention. Taylor wished she could trust Tristan enough to leave him alone in her back yard, but she'd seen how high he could jump trying to peer over the fence and his middle name was Houdini so she didn't dare. No telling where a search for adventure would lead him if he managed to escape.

Taylor put the kettle on and rinsed the teapot as Edie set out cookies and muffins on a plate.

"What an afternoon!" Taylor said as they settled across from each other at Edie's oak table.

"The sale went well," agreed Edie.

"I was actually referring to the sideshows," said Taylor.

"I thought you might be," Edie grinned. "You got to hear all the opinions from your vantage point. And I even saw Andrew make an appearance."

"Yes. He brought the change back after Brenda had volunteered to get it. That was happening number one. Brenda was so anxious to leave as though the change gave her an excuse. Then she never came back. She told Andrew she had an errand to run when she met him. But she still hadn't returned when we closed up. I wonder where she went."

"Probably a simple explanation. Maybe she suddenly remembered she was out of bread."

"At a bake sale?" Edie chuckled in response and explained. "You know what I mean—some staple she needed for dinner tonight."

"It wouldn't have seemed so strange if she hadn't asked earlier about the black book."

"What black book?"

"A fictional one as far as I know. She wanted to know if Jonah had a black book with him when I found him. She said he had landscaping plans for her back garden in it. But that's not all." Taylor took a break to swallow half an oatmeal and raisin cookie before going on.

"She wasn't the only one to ask about a black book. Maggie Trent asked about it too. She also gave some excuse about estimates for the house she's fixing up."

"Hmmm." said Edie. "One person looking for it might be only passing strange but two.... I think you'd better tell Andrew about it."

"Speak of the devil," said Taylor as Andrew's familiar staccato knock came to Edie's door.

"Come in Andrew," Edie called without getting up. "In the kitchen."

Andrew appeared round the corner but pulled up short when he saw Taylor. "Oh, I didn't know you'd be here. I didn't see your car."

"I parked in the back lane out of the sun. Besides, why would you assume I'd drive the whole block from my house to Edie's?"

"Sorry." Andrew grinned sheepishly. "You just surprised me, that's all."

Taylor got another mug from the cupboard and Edie waved at the plate of calories on the table. "Help yourself," she said.

"Don't mind if I do," said Andrew, promptly demolishing a muffin in about two bites before reaching for a second.

"I just stopped in to talk about Monty," he said to Edie.

"Is someone claiming him?"

"Doesn't look like anyone in the family wants him and we're done with him, forensics—wise, so if you know of anyone who would like to adopt him, he could do with a good home."

"Someone owes Edie for boarding him," piped up Taylor. "Where does she send the bill?"

"This one is a freebie, I think, Taylor," said Edie. "If no—one wants him, no one is going to pay for his keep." Edie ran the boarding kennel more as a hobby than a business.

"But you're in the business of boarding dogs," said Andrew, "So if you make up a bill, I'll pass it on to Melvin Donovan. He's looking after Jonah's legal issues; I'm sure he'll see it's paid."

Taylor realized later that she had missed the golden opportunity to suggest Andrew would be a good match for Monty, but other ideas pushed themselves forward.

"Speaking of Donovan," she began, with a glance at Edie, "I've had a few unusual conversations about finding Jonah I should tell you about."

"Now why am I not surprised?"

She glared at him for a second and went on. "Jonah seems to have written down a lot of things in a black notebook. People seem to think I know where it is and want to know it's whereabouts."

"That's easy," said Andrew. "We have it."

"You do?"

"Yes. It was in the truck, fallen down under the seat. We found it when we gave the truck a once—over." He leaned forward, elbows on the table. "I think you'd better tell me who was interested in the book."

"Well for starters, Brenda Prentiss. She asked me about it today at the bake sale."

Andrew nodded with a thoughtful look. " Yes, I think that fits with one of the notes."

"And." prompted Taylor.

"And nothing. There's no reason for you to know."

"I'm telling you everything I know," protested Taylor.

"And I thank you for that. But I'm police and you're private citizen so the need to know is a little different. Now go on. Who else was asking about the book?"

Taylor gave in. "Maggie Trent."

"Maggie Trent?" Andrew seemed surprised.

"Yes." She glanced at Edie who nodded in Andrew's direction. "I'd better tell you what happened when I took Tristan for a walk yesterday. I think it will explain her interest."

She related the story of her eavesdropping at Jonah's house and was gratified to see Andrew's mouth wriggle with a suppressed grin.

"That would explain one of the notations," he said when she had finished relating the story.

"Notations? So he did write things down in his book."

"Of course," said Andrew. "That's why he carried it

around in the truck. He doesn't seem to have been into computers. All his jobs were noted in the book along with dates completed and money received."

"And a lot more, I bet," said Taylor.

"He did have a section in the back that contained cryptic notes, along with initials." Andrew then clamped his mouth shut as though regretting his words.

"Aha!" said Taylor. "There you have your motive—or motives."

Edie flashed her a warning glance but it was too late.

Andrew stood up. "Taylor, you don't need to tell me my job. I'm well aware of Jonah's little side business."

"I'm sorry. That's not what I meant. Sit down, please. You haven't finished your muffin."

Andrew held her gaze in an angry glare a moment longer, then sat down.

"I'm not trying to interfere, honestly. I'm just trying to be a good citizen and let the police know what I've seen and heard. That's what I'm supposed to do right?"

Andrew shook his head. "Why is it you always take civic duty to a different level than the rest of the public?"

"My burning desire to help? My overzealous conscience?"

"Curiosity bug, more likely." Andrew seemed mollified. Maybe the muffins helped.

"Okay, okay. You're right," said Andrew. "The back section of the notebook is obviously not about odd jobs. It's impossible what he was trying to say from the squiggles he made. They were meant to jog his memory, not to explain to anyone else, so we'll never know most of them. The initials—well, in a town this size we might figure them out, but even in Badger Lake do you have any idea how many J.L's there are?"

"J.L.?" mused Taylor.

"It wasn't a real set of initials," said Andrew. "I was just reaching for an example." He ignored her disappointed expression.

"I know there are lots of people with reason to dislike him. But you're not going to tell me that a sexual encounter of a rather bizarre nature or a bit of a past you'd like hidden is enough reason to kill a man. Give him a thrashing, threaten to report him, yes. But murder—it's a bit of a stretch."

"But they must have been willing to give him a few dollars here and there to shut him up." Taylor persisted.

"A few dollars, yes. But I don't think he dug that deeply. And I don't think anyone in Badger Lake has anything that dark to hide. Maybe they figured a few bucks here and there was worth it to shut him up. But I think he knew his limits. If he got too greedy, I'm sure all his customers would tell him 'publish and be damned.'"

"Maybe it's something personal." suggested Taylor after she determined Andrew wasn't going to be more forthcoming about the initials. "He has a reputation as a ladies' man. Maybe a married woman? Maybe an angry husband or boyfriend? It could be a crime of passion."

"Quit reading so many detective novels, Taylor." Andrew was over his annoyance and back to amused.

"I don't really. I read biographies mostly."

"Hmmph," said Andrew with an unconvinced air.

"Children!" said Taylor suddenly.

"What?" Both Edie and Andrew jumped at her sudden exclamation.

"Well, it seems to be a known fact that he had an affair with Danika long ago and Franny is his child. Maybe there are more we don't know about. He seems to have scattered his seed widely." Edie laughed outright at the biblical expression.

Taylor went on. "Maybe a mother or child is out to get something back from him they feel entitled to—like any money he has, or his house. Maybe they feel they're due and would have a claim on it."

"You forget Taylor, that the house didn't belong to Jonah. And as for money—well, I think he spent as quickly as he received."

"Gambler?"

"Not in casinos, but the word is he liked to bet on horses."

"Mm. But maybe no one knew he didn't own the house. We didn't."

"I think if someone were going to kill Jonah for his house they would have looked into the ownership first."

"I wonder why Danika tried so hard to get Jonah to pay support for Franny and even had him on the birth certificate and then suddenly gave up."

"Maybe she decided she didn't want him in her child's life." offered Edie.

"Or," Taylor wrinkled her brow in thought. "Maybe Jonah wasn't really the father." She straightened up in her chair, running with the idea. "It's so easy to get a DNA test done now. Maybe Jonah insisted and discovered he wasn't the father after all and she had to back off."

"You just eliminated a motive, then," said Edie. Taylor looked up at Andrew as he stood so quickly his chair scraped the floor.

"I'm off," he said with no further comment and headed for the door. "Thanks for the tea and muffins," he threw over his shoulder as he opened the door.

"Well, what got into him?" said Taylor. "What did I say? Or rather what did I say that was any worse than the rest of the conversation?"

Edie looked thoughtful. "I don't know." she said slowly.

"Do you think something I said gave him an idea about the case?"

"No. I think whatever bit him was on more of a personal level."

"Well, now you can see what I mean about Andrew behaving strangely these days."

Edie stood with her hand on the teapot. "I need to add more water."

"Not for me," said Taylor. "I'd better go."

Edie finished rinsing the teapot and turned to Taylor. "I think you'd better talk to Andrew soon."

"What were we just doing?"

"I mean a one on one talk. Something is definitely bothering him and I think it concerns you."

"Easier said than done. Andrew seems to be avoiding one on one situations with me. In a group he's his old self but alone..."

"All the more reason to talk."

Taylor silently agreed. She'd need to make a plan to get Andrew alone. It probably wasn't going to happen till he got this murder sorted. It gave him a ready excuse to make quick exits.

She distracted herself by calling Jimmy. He promised to come Monday morning to look at what had to be done to update the house. Taylor told herself this wasn't a commitment. Getting an estimate didn't mean she'd actually do the reno.

Chapter
Fourteen

Sunday morning Taylor decided to go to Church. She wasn't a weekly attendee, but tried to make an appearance at least once a month. It had been longer than that since her last service.

Tristan fooled around so long over his morning routine that she was one of the last to arrive, just making it into a rear pew before the first hymn.

She felt strangely disappointed after the service not to receive the barrage of questions about Jonah that she expected. She should feel relieved, not disappointed. Apparently the congregation felt gossip belonged in the Northland, not in church. Instead the after service chatter centred around the bake sale, its success and plans for a summer concert.

The day was one of those clouds one minute—not the next—days, but they were mainly light and fluffy ones, with no portent of rain.

After a quick lunch, she sat over a cup of coffee wondering about her renos. If Jimmy gave her a good estimate, she was going to go ahead, but without the decorating skills of Maggie. With Darcy's help, she should be able to work out colour schemes that would work, cabinets that functioned and bathroom fixtures that were useful rather than trendy.

She stirred at the feel of wet nose on her leg. "Right, old boy," she said. "A walk will do us both good."

She followed her usual route with the odd sideline as Tristan spotted a shrub or bird he wanted to investigate. It was a lovely lazy hazy Sunday and she intended to enjoy it in a spirit of contentment and relaxation. No more thoughts of either Jonah or renos.

She should have changed her route. Jonah of course sprang into her mind as she neared his house. The For Sale sign was in the ground now and the truck still sat in the driveway.

A movement caught her eye. Someone or something was behind the truck. Maybe Maggie had a prospective buyer. Sundays weren't days of rest for real estate agents. They were sometimes the best option for showing properties to people who worked long weekly hours. No sign of Maggie's van though. No sign of any vehicle other than Jonah's. As she passed on the far side of the street, a figure stood up behind the truck and turned a startled gaze in her direction.

Hank! What was he doing here? Nothing legitimate, it seemed, as he turned quickly without acknowledging her and disappeared along the side of the house to the back lane.

Could Hank be another of Jonah's victims? If so, he and anyone else looking for incriminating evidence were out of luck. The police had found the black book and probably anything else of interest.

So much for keeping Jonah out of her thoughts today.

As she rounded the corner, she nearly ran into Brenda, two white miniature poodles in tow. She was a long way from home in her walk. Taylor couldn't remember running into her here before.

Brenda was, for once, not dressed like a fifties sit-com housewife. She was wearing jeans and a short-sleeved flowered blouse. Taylor would have sworn Brenda's closet didn't even contain a pair of jeans.

The dogs circled each other and carried on doggie conversations. Taylor was about to move on with a smiling "Good morning," but Brenda showed signs of wanting to talk.

They discussed the bake sale and the weather but finally came to the end of anything Taylor could think of as holding mutual interest.

Brenda suddenly blurted out, "Could I talk with you for a bit, Taylor?"

Taylor refrained from answering "That's what I thought we were doing," and said instead, "Sure. Would you like to have coffee at the Northland? We'd have to take the dogs home first. Or you could come to my place. I still have some of those bake sale cookies."

Brenda shuddered when she mentioned the Northland. "No, not there," she said. "it was actually a private word I wanted with you. Could we go to my house instead? Steven is out doing a round of visiting this afternoon so we'll be alone." They turned and headed for Brenda's home. The walk seemed endless to Taylor. Brenda marched along, tugging at her dogs' leads when they hesitated or attempted to go off—path. She offered no conversation and Taylor was at a loss for small—talk so she just followed in Brenda's wake. The sidewalks were narrow enough that two people walking abreast with three dogs was a daunting task, so Taylor allowed herself to slip back a few steps. It looked as though they weren't even walking together, merely happened to be dog-walking in the same direction. Maybe that's what Brenda wanted.

She followed her into a well-kept front yard and around the side to the back door. The lawn was neatly mowed, the flowers well-tended and the entire garden seemed to echo love and care. There was only one bare spot on the lawn, near a back gate; Brenda must have her dogs trained to do their duties in a single spot. She looked down at Tristan— good luck trying to train him along that path.

Brenda checked to be sure the side gate was shut and unleashed her dogs. Taylor followed suit. Tristan began to roll in the grass, wriggling in ecstasy.

"In here," said Brenda. "We'll have tea in the kitchen if that's all right. It's much cooler on this side of the house. For some reason, the air-conditioning isn't working properly."

She motioned for Taylor to sit at a banquette that formed the seating for a large kitchen table. "Maybe a cold drink would be better than tea. Do you like lemonade?"

Drinks poured, Brenda took a seat across from Taylor. She ran her finger around her glass, making tracks in the condensation.

Taylor was never good at sitting in silence, but she forced herself. Obviously Brenda had something momentous on her mind and would come to it in her own good time. She glanced around the kitchen. She'd been in the house several times but never in the kitchen. It was homier than the rest of the house, with brightly coloured pottery, a collection of old teapots along the top cupboard, and dog beds and dishes in their own little corner by the door.

She finally spoke, "When you found Jonah..."

Taylor groaned. She hoped the sound was internal, not audible. Of course she should have known that was what was on Brenda's mind.

"Was he still alive? Did he say anything?"

"No on both counts. I tried to find a pulse and couldn't. He was definitely dead."

"And you're sure there was no notebook or anything on him? Or in the truck?"

"I told you before, Brenda, there was nothing I could see. I wasn't looking. I just wanted to get out of there and get help as quickly as I could."

"Of course. I just thought you might have seen something."

"Brenda, if you're worried about something, you should talk to the police. If there was a notebook or anything of that nature, they'll have it. I wouldn't have touched anything even if it was there."

Brenda sat motionless, still playing with her glass, but a tear rolled down her cheek and splashed on the table. Still she sat.

Taylor reached across the table and touched her hand. "What is it, Brenda? what's wrong?"

The tears began coming faster now. Suddenly Brenda lunged forward and sobbed into her arms which she crossed on the table to form a cradle for her head.

Taylor rose and went around to the other side of the table. She sat beside Brenda and patted her on the shoulder, not knowing what else to do. It was so out of character for Brenda to show emotion in public.

Finally Brenda sat up and reached into her pocket for a tissue. She rubbed her eyes and blew her nose and looked up sheepishly at Taylor. "You must think I've gone crazy."

"No, just deeply troubled by something. Is there anything I can do to help? This revolves around Jonah somehow, doesn't it?"

"Taylor, I'm going to tell you a story, but you have to

swear not to repeat it to another soul."

"Of course." Taylor hoped it wasn't a promise she'd regret. What if Brenda was going to confess to some horrible crime? A terrible thought hit her. What if she was going to admit she killed Jonah?

"Brenda, are you sure I'm the one you should be talking to?"

"Not really," she said. "But I have to tell someone. You'll do as well as anyone."

She took another sniff into the tissue and slipped it back into her pocket.

"The trouble all along has been keeping secrets. If I had talked about it years ago, there would have been no problem now."

"Jonah was blackmailing you, wasn't he?"

Brenda nodded. "It was all so stupid. I should have ignored him. I should have told him to go to hell, that I didn't care who he told," It was a sign of her distress that the expletive slipped out easily and unapologetically. "I should have stood up in the church one Sunday morning and told the whole town. Maybe I will, but first I have to tell Steven." The tears began to come again, but quietly and singly. "I can practise with you."

Taylor felt relief. If Brenda was serious, it meant secret—keeping and she'd never been good at that. Not the way her brother Greg had been. The secret he kept... she forced her mind back to Brenda.

"Taylor something bad happened to me years ago. Before I married Steven. Before I met him even."

She took a deep breath. "I was raped. I was late coming home from a Young People's Meeting and I was walking alone. I should have called my parents for a ride, but it was a small town, a safe town I thought, and a short walk. He came out of nowhere—from a back alley. He had a knife and he pulled me down the lane and into an old shed. Then he raped me."

Taylor moved her chair closer to Brenda's and held her left hand in hers. She made no comment, not wanting to staunch the flow of words.

"They never did catch the person who did it. He had a balaclava on and I couldn't identify him. Another girl was attacked a couple of weeks later but she managed to get away. Then nothing! The police said he probably got scared the second time at nearly getting caught and moved on somewhere else. I was almost relieved that they didn't catch him. It meant not having to go to court or talk about it to anyone. Then I felt so guilty because it meant some other girl was going through what I did."

She paused and Taylor said, "I can't imagine what you must have gone through." She couldn't think of any comforting words, and besides, Brenda didn't seem to be looking for comforting words.

"That wasn't the end of it," said Brenda. "I got pregnant."

Taylor had no answer for that one. She couldn't come out and ask where the baby was now, could she?

"With what had happened to me, it was pretty difficult to get away from it in a small town, so Dad applied for a transfer—he was a bank manager—and got one to a town far enough away no one would know about what happened to me. But then, with the pregnancy it was still a problem in a new town since I wasn't married. Oh I know," she waved off any protest Taylor might make, "It isn't such a big thing now to be a single parent, but my family were old-fashioned and it did make a difference to them."

"So, I went off to visit a cousin on the coast and have the baby. Mom and Dad insisted I give it up. I didn't argue because I didn't see any way of raising a child on my own and I didn't know if I could live with the knowledge that my child was the result of something so awful. Every time I looked at him, I was afraid I'd see only his father and the horrible brute he was. It wouldn't be a loving home that he deserved."

"It was a boy?"

"Yes. A perfect little boy. I only had time for a moment with him before he was gone. Gone forever."

"But how could Jonah find out about this? Did you know him then? Did he live in your town?"

"No. The adoption was private. Mom and Dad looked after it. Before I signed the papers, I made the lawyer give a condition." She stopped to give a swipe at her eyes with a clean tissue. "The parents send me a letter once a year on his birthday through the lawyer and tell me how he is doing.

They also send a picture. In return, I promise not to contact them."

"But someday, maybe he'll look for you? What then?"

"Maybe he will. He's only eight now."

"But Jonah? He found the letters!" she said with sudden clarification.

"Yes. He was doing some work in the bathroom. I was coming out of the bedroom. I thought he'd gone. I had the box with me where I kept the letters and the picture. It was an old box meant for a diary. I had it since I was a little girl. It locked and Steven would never think to pry into it."

"Anyhow," she went on, "I had the box in my hand. I thought I was alone in the house and I wanted to reread the last letter."

"But how would Jonah know there was something important there?"

"My expression, I guess. He gave me a strange look-over— the way he does to all women, I guess. He likes married women, I'm told. So he must have guessed by the way I grabbed the box there was something in there. I turned and ran into the bedroom and locked the door. I stayed there until he'd left."

"But he had to come again. I asked Steven to get someone else. I didn't want to be in the house when he came. But I couldn't explain why. I just made sure I wasn't around when Jonah came."

"That was my big mistake. He was alone in the house and he must have started searching. It wasn't him I should have been afraid of, it was his prying eyes. He found the box, opened it and took one of the letters. Then he asked for money to get it back."

"And that's what you hoped he had with him so you could get it back."

"Yes. I should have told Steven long ago. But somehow I was afraid he'd judge me for giving the baby away. I should have known better. Steven isn't the judgmental type. But as time went on it got more difficult. We never had kids, you see, and I wondered if something happened to me then. No one told me anything went wrong, but I felt guilty for that."

Taylor wondered if that guilt was what lay behind the perfect housewife syndrome Brenda seemed to display. If she felt responsible for them not having a family, maybe she wanted to make it up to him by being the model wife and homemaker.

"The time has come," said Brenda. She stood up as though dismissing Taylor and the part she'd played in the catharsis. Taylor felt obliged to stand as well. She hated to leave Brenda in her present state, but it appeared she wasn't wanted any longer.

"Remember you promised." Taylor felt Brenda's eyes lock onto hers. "Don't tell any-one."

"Of course I won't. but you are going to, aren't you?"

"In my own good time."

A car's tires crunched on the gravel at the side of the house. "That will be Steven now," Brenda said. "He always uses the back door. Go out the front door please, before he comes in. And remember, not a word to anyone."

She practically shoved Taylor out of the house. Taylor began to push the front door closed behind her the same moment she could hear the back door open and Steven's "Honey, I'm home."

She still had to slip around the back way to collect Tristan. Brenda must have forgotten that. Then she looked down at her hands and realized his leash was still on the bench in the kitchen. It was going to be a long walk home. without a leash, Tristan would become a jumping bean, stopping to sniff and examine everything and explore each lane and garden on the way home.

Edie was at the Boarding Kennel when she and Tristan arrived home. She could see the front door open and hear Edie's voice inside. Thinking she had a customer Taylor was going to bypass the kennel. Tristan, happily off leash, had other ideas. Taylor ran after him and found Edie, not with a human customer, but talking to a chocolate Labrador who jumped at the advent of a yapping Jack Russell, but in true Lab style, quickly offered a friendly nose to Tristan.

"Sorry Edie, I left his leash at Brenda's and he's a terror off-lead."

She could see Edie's eyebrows rise at the tidbit of where she'd been, but she decided to wait till the dogs were settled to tell her as much, or as little as she felt she could. Promises were a confining thing when faced with gossip or murder.

"New customer, I see."

"His family are off at the Lake and didn't take into account how much a Lab gets into fishing or anything to do with water. They decided to leave him here for the rest of their visit." She rubbed the Lab's ears. "Well get along just fine won't we, Brownie?"

"Original name," sniffed Taylor.

"Apparently it's a play on his 'chocolate' heritage and not a mere comment on his colour."

"Tea?"

"I'll be over in a few minutes. I'm going to put Brownie right next to Monty. I want to see how they get along with the fence between them. Maybe I can walk them together. It would do Monty good to have a friend."

Taylor slipped away with Tristan. She was glad she had more than one leash. She'd hate to go back so soon to retrieve her forgotten one. Who knows what she could be interrupting.

She put the kettle on to boil and dished out some treats left—over from the bake sale.

It wasn't long before there was a quick tap on the door and a "I'm here," in Edie's alto.

"I didn't know you and Brenda were coffee buddies," Edie said when they'd poured and taken the first sips.

"I ran into her walking Tristan and she asked me in," Taylor began, trying to phrase her narrative with an eye to keeping confidences but still imparting information. She decided with Edie the best approach was straight on.

"She told me a story in confidence and I promised not to tell anyone."

"Well then, of course, you can't" said Edie simply. "Did her story make you discount her from our list of suspects?"

Taylor grinned at that. They didn't officially have a list of suspects. Last year, when faced with a series of crimes Taylor was caught up in, they had made a list of possibles and added pros and cons for each. This was a little different. Last year involved Taylor personally. Today she was merely an unfortunate person who had found a body.

"Weren't you telling me only short hours ago to stay out of things and leave it to Andrew?"

"I was. I meant to stay out of the investigation. That doesn't mean we can't speculate in the safety of our own homes."

"You should have been a lawyer," said Taylor. Edie shuddered at the thought.

"No thank you. Trying to teach the young of Badger Lake to count without using their fingers and make a complete sentence without the word 'like' was good enough for me."

"Do you miss it? Teaching, I mean."

"Sometimes. But I'm content with my retired—well semi-retired—life now."

"Oh," said Taylor suddenly. "I ran into someone else on my walk today. Before I ran into Brenda."

Edie looked at her expectantly. "Who?"

"Hank. I didn't run into him exactly, but I saw him. He tried hard not to see me. He was skulking, that's the only word that describes it, skulking, around Jonah's truck."

"The police had the truck. They would have gone over it thoroughly, I don't know what Hank could possibly think he'd find."

"Well he scuttled when he saw me. So he was up to no good."

Taylor chewed and swallowed a chunk of chocolate chip cookie. "These are still good," she said. "Back to Hank. Do you think he and Kelly are having problems? He keeps showing up looking for her at the oddest times and she's looking a bit frazzled. Do you think there's trouble in paradise?"

"I don't think their marriage was ever paradise," said Edie. "Probably none are, but theirs had baggage from the start."

"Oh, you mean the fact that Hank already had two kids. Kelly was rather young to take on a ready—made family." She thought about it. "I think there's more to it than that. Oh! I just remembered she used to go out with Jonah. Before she met Hank. Maybe that's why she's been acting strangely. Maybe she still had some feelings for him."

"If she did, she's one of the few people in town." Edie cradled her cup and said slowly," I saw Hank and Kelly, a few weeks ago, in the Post office, having a bit of a row."

Taylor prompted, "Do you mean an argument or a physical row?"

"Maybe a bit of both. Kelly had picked up the mail and had opened an envelope when I walked into the mailbox vestibule. Hank snatched it from her and told her to mind her own business. It was addressed to him. He grabbed her by the arm and practically shoved her outside."

"Poor Kelly! I remember seeing bruises on her last week. But I never thought much of it. Look at me. I'm always getting black and blue marks, but I manage to give them to myself without any help. But if Hank is being abusive, Kelly isn't the type to confide in anyone. Does she have any one to confide in? No parents, no siblings, and she seems not to have any close friends."

"Those could be the markers for a situation of abuse— Isolation, overprotectiveness. On the other hand we don't know enough about what goes on behind closed doors to make snap judgments."

"Is there anything we can do?"

"Not unless Kelly wants us to. We can try to talk to her, offer her a shoulder, but not much more than that."

"Do you think if we interfered it would make things worse?"

"Quite possibly. Besides, we don't know for sure he's being abusive. The jury is still out on any bruises she has had and the argument in the post office wasn't that much worse than that of other couples I've seen that blew over." She paused for effect and said, "I didn't tell you everything about that encounter."

"There's more?" If Taylor were like Tristan, her ears would be pricked straight up.

"Hank threw the envelope on the floor of the Post Office when he took the letter. After they'd gone I picked up the envelope to throw it in the trash. I couldn't help but see the return address and the logo. "

"And?"

"It was a medical emblem. And the return address was a lab. A private lab."

"One of them is sick?"

"I don't know. It was strange they'd get information from a private lab. Why not through the clinic?"

"Hank strikes me as a suspicious sort of person. The kind who believes all sorts of conspiracy theories. Maybe he's double checking something his doctor told him."

"Could be. But why hide it from Kelly?"

"Maybe she's the one who's sick and he did it on the sly, not wanting to worry her."

"Hmmph! I can't see Hank being that sensitive. Especially the way her treated her."

Chapter
Fifteen

On Monday morning Taylor rose early to be sure her house was in shape for Jimmy. True to his word, he arrived early. Felix, his boxer, came in at his heels. Jimmy knew Taylor wouldn't mind a dog visitor. When he and Tristan began to get a little rowdy, she shooed them into the back yard to play.

Jimmy wandered the house, taking measurements which he wrote down on an iPad, 'hmmming' a lot as he made the rounds.

"I want to start small," Taylor said. "Only one room at a time. I thought maybe the bathroom first?"

"If it were me, I'd start with the kitchen." Jimmy said. "Needs a total refit." He stopped to look at the doorway. "You could pull down that wall and make it open—concept," he said.

"No", said Taylor. "I want to keep the kitchen separate. It works best for me that way. It's an eat—in kitchen so my visitors are handy while I cook anyway."

"Hmm" mumbled Jimmy. "Probably for the best all around." He patted the wall in question. "It's a load-bearing wall, so you'd need pillars anyhow."

She shuddered. "No thanks"

"Separate kitchen it is then," he said.

"Can you give me an estimate for both the bathroom and kitchen. Then I'll decide which one to start on.

"I'll have something for you by the end of the week,"

'You must be busier than ever now," said Taylor, "With Jonah gone," she added when Jimmy appeared puzzled at the comment.

"Oh, aye. I see what you mean. You were the one that found him, weren't you?"

"Yes," said Taylor simply, waiting to see what information Jimmy might part with. He didn't follow the town trend of gossip. Instead he said, "I hope you don't make it a habit, lass. This finding bodies. People will start to avoid you." He chuckled at his own joke and Taylor pasted on an answering smile.

She went to the back door to corral the dogs.

She ran into Andrew again at the Post Office. Well, not exactly ran into. She was only out for a quick morning walk with Tristan. He'd already had his main exercise with Jimmy's dog, and she wasn't even planning to check for mail, wasn't expecting anything as usual. But when she saw Andrew's vehicle parked outside, she made a deliberate turn into the building and headed for the mailboxes. Maybe she could invite him for coffee and have that heart to heart.

Andrew was scanning his mail, dumping them individually into the wastebasket.

"Strange, the amount of junk mail we still get, isn't it? You'd think they would have all reverted to spam by now."

Andrew obviously hadn't seen her arrive as he jumped at least a foot when she began to speak. He quickly recovered and agreed with her comment. "You're right," he said. "Five pieces of mail and not one keeper in the lot." He dusted his hands as though ridding himself of the vestiges of trash and headed for the door. End of conversation.

So much for any plan she had to get a private discussion with Andrew. His hasty departure seemed to indicate whatever was troubling him had something to do with mail, either received or expected. Expected, she decided, because he hadn't left with even one letter. What could he possibly be looking for in the mail? And how did it affect their relationship? It seemed she wasn't going to find out today.

She left without bothering to open her mailbox. Even Tristan looked a little put out that one of his favourite people had ignored him.

Taylor continued past the Co-op, cutting through the lot on the way home. She could see Kelly through the glass doors at the front check—out and, catching her eye, gave a friendly wave.

"Okay, home with you," she said to Tristan. "I'm in the mood for coffee and gossip." She dropped him off and grabbed her purse. It was late into coffee time at the Northland and she guessed Edie would be there. She wondered if the topics of conversation would have moved on from Jonah to Saturday's Bake Sale. Not likely.

As it turned out, Edie was a no—show—or maybe she had already left. The crowd was thinning. The first people she saw were Darcy and Dan who waved her over. Dan was in a conversation with two other men across the aisle so Taylor slipped in across from Darcy.

"How's it going?" she asked, nodding in the direction of Darcy's abdomen.

"So far, so good. I haven't had any morning sickness. My cousin Jenna said she couldn't stand the smell or taste of coffee her whole pregnancy. I don't know how I'd cope if that happened to me."

"Tea. Plenty of strong tea for the caffeine fix. It likely won't though. Everyone is different, they say. You could be one of the lucky ones."

"From your mouth to God's ear. Andrew was in a while ago. He sat with us but kept looking at his watch and took off."

"Probably something to do with the murder case. Maybe an appointment. I saw him in the post office a few minutes ago."

"He seems a little distracted. I see what you mean about him being different. But then, it's likely that a murder under his nose would have an effect."

Changing topics she said, "Are you going to the funeral this afternoon?"

"I don't think so," said Taylor. "Considering the circumstances, it would probably be a distraction if I went. Everyone seems to want information from me that I don't have. Are you?"

Darcy shook her head. "I feel guilty about it because I usually attend funerals if I know the people. But I think I'd feel uncomfortable at this one, like the sole kid at an adult party."

"I know how you feel." Taylor looked around the coffee

shop. "I wonder how many of these will be going." She wasn't expecting an answer and didn't get one.

Darcy and Dan had been in the coffee shop before she arrived and she could see Dan was getting antsy when his friends across the way left. He was one of those men who had difficulty sitting unless they were occupied. She took pity on him and, after a quick finish to her coffee, said, "Well, I have some work to get done. Jimmy was over this morning. He's giving me a quote on some renos and I'd better start preparing for the work."

"Are you going to ask Maggie for advice?"

Taylor grimaced. "A little niggle on that front," she said. "I think I'm going to do it on my own with the help of a lot home improvement magazines." Dan was already standing, ready to be on his way. Darcy rolled her eyes at him and said. "Well, looks like we're leaving too."

"Oh sorry," said Dan. "I should have asked if you were finished." he leaned over to kiss the top of her head.

"I am now," said Darcy.

"Can I pick your brain too for design ideas?"

"Of course. Come on over for coffee this week and we'll have an afternoon of browsing through pages of design. On second thought, considering the state of our living room, I'll bring the books to you."

"Good idea. Thanks. Any day you have the time."

Taylor made a detour on the way home to the drug store to pick up some body wash and shampoo. On the way out she saw Anna getting into the driver's side of a red Focus parked in front. Anna saw her too and aborted her plan. She stepped onto the sidewalk.

"I took your advice," she said.

Taylor looked at her questioningly. "What advice?"

"To beard the lion in his den."

"Oh, your father. Did you have any luck?"

"Not the type of luck I hoped for. He was his usual miserable self and laughed at me when I asked him. He was in one of his more lucid moments though, because he certainly grasped what I was asking him."

"He wouldn't tell you?"

"He said I was as stupid as my mother if I thought he'd raise someone else's brat as his own. That, like it or not, I was his."

"So you have your answer?"

"Not exactly. Then he went on to talk about Jonah being a true son to him, and smirking as he said it. I still have my doubts. I think he figured out what I hoped for and told me the opposite just to be mean."

Then she reached into her pocket for a small piece of paper. "But I may get the better of him yet. I snuck some hair from his brush and I'm going to get them tested for DNA."

"Is that legal?" asked Taylor.

Anna snorted. "I'm not going to be presenting the findings in court. I only want to know if he's my real father."

"You mean you want to know that he's not your real father."

"You're right there. I don't even care if I find out who my genetic father is. I just want to be sure it's not that old sod that raised me. And now I will." she flashed the paper in front of Taylor's face.

"I went to school with Trish, the pharmacy assistant. She gave me the address of a private lab. I'm going to have the test done. It's going to cost a few bucks but it will be worth it."

Taylor managed a quick glance at the small sheet of paper. There was a logo with a name and phone number. It looked as though it had been torn from a larger page, perhaps a letterhead. The design reminded her of Edie's description of the envelope she had picked up after her encounter with Hank and Kelly in the post office.

Anna disappeared back into the Focus and Taylor was left to muse on the way home about the significance of the lab logo.

Was Hank unsure about his paternity of the twins? Was that the test he was having done? It would explain why he was so angry at the thought Kelly might open the envelope first. He wanted to have proof and then confront her. Or maybe confrontation wasn't the object of the test. Maybe he only wanted to know.

She was nearly home when she caught a glimpse of movement next door at the kennel.

Edie heard her too and turned to wave. "Monty is getting his mojo back," she said. "I'm tuckered out. He's far more active than Jasper ever was. And Brownie is no slouch either."

"Goes with the breed, I guess. When did you ever see a couch potato border collie? Come on over for coffee when you have Monty and Brownie settled. I never got my second cup at the Northland."

Tristan gave a bark. "I'd better go before he gets into full chorus," she said. "He hears the dogs. He'll be ready for another play date. Do you think we should bring Monty along too?"

Edie hesitated. "I think I'll wait on that. He knows Jasper and Brownie now and they get along great, but—might be better to have him one on one with Tristan first."

"Okay. I'll put the coffee on." Tristan gave her a quick welcome and then stared behind her with a disappointed look. He was expecting company. Denver merely gave her a cat look that said 'Oh were you gone? I hadn't noticed. You might want to do something about my food dish.'

Coffee ready and dogs playing in the back yard, Edie settled at the table and held her cup of brew.

"I just ran into Andrew in the post office," Taylor said.

"Did you get a chance to talk to him?"

"He didn't look to be in a talking mood. Besides when I do talk to him I want him somewhere I can corner him and he can't escape."

"Yes," drawled Edie. "Kidnapping has always worked well in romance."

"You know what I mean. Oh, and in front of the drug store I ran into Anna. You know—Jonah's sister."

"I thought she would have left town. Maybe she decided to stay for the funeral."

"Nope. She's still here. And I have some information. One mystery is solved." She thought for a moment and added. "Maybe not solved—maybe just opening onto another mystery."

"You're rambling, Taylor. What did Anna say?"

"I told you she thinks her father isn't her father." She stopped to ponder her remark. "That didn't come out right but you know what I mean. Anyhow she went to the Care Home to talk to him—her father that is."

"I don't imagine she got very far. Neil never was the

most cooperative of souls and now I imagine he isn't aware a lot of the time."

"She said he was pretty lucid when she was there. But you're right about the co-operative part. He wouldn't tell her anything. But she decided to see for herself. She took some hair from his brush when he wasn't looking and she's sending it off along with her own DNA to a private lab for testing."

"I wonder what she'll do if it proves he isn't her father?"

"She says she doesn't care—as long as it's not him."

"That's what she says—now."

"But that's not the point of the story. She got the address for a lab to do the testing—from one of the girls at the pharmacy. She showed me the name. It was torn off a sheet of letterhead I think. And," Taylor stopped here to be sure she had Edie's attention.

"And—it's the logo you described to me from the envelope Hank dropped on the floor. That's what Hank was doing. He was trying to find out if he really was the father of the boys!"

She sat back to watch Edie's reaction. It wasn't exactly as she had hoped. Edie sat contemplating, her eyes on a spot over Taylor's head.

"That doesn't bode well," she said.

"No. It doesn't. Poor Kelly if it turned out Hank isn't the father. Maybe that's why she got those bruises."

"We don't know what the results were. Maybe he was wrong and he is the father. Hank always was a bit paranoid. He loves conspiracy theories and I remember he got into a bar fight once with someone who he thought said something off about Kelly."

"But if he isn't..."

"Then I think maybe Andrew should be given the information we have."

"But he told me to butt out."

"That's not the same thing as withholding information. Taylor, this is important. Because if Hank isn't the father of the twins, you know who probably was?"

"Jonah!"

"Precisely. Kelly had a short fling with him before she married Hank. And Hank knew about it and so did everyone else in town."

"So he has a motive to kill Jonah!"

"Along with half the town, don't forget. But still, Andrew probably won't know and we have to tell him."

"Don't look at me! I think it would be better coming from you. He's much more likely to take you seriously. Coming from me, he'll shake his head and mutter about my overactive imagination."

"Not in this case, Taylor. But if you like, I'll tell him. If I can catch him this afternoon...No, I remember he said something about being out of town this afternoon."

"Out of town where?"

"I don't know. He didn't say. Something to do with the case, I imagine. I'll catch him tomorrow morning."

"You could leave a message or talk to Joe at the station."

"I think person to person is best. The fewer people that hear this the better. If it turns out to be totally irrelevant to Andrew's investigation, we don't want to run the risk of ruining Kelly's reputation with idle talk."

Taylor fell back, crestfallen. "Of course," she said. "I wasn't thinking of it that way."

She decided to change gears. "Let's talk about something else for a change. I'm getting suddenly sick and tired of Jonah. Did I tell you about my plans for reno?"

She watched Edie's face for her reaction. Edie had spent a lot of time here with Aunt Grace. It was like another home to her. Maybe she'd be upset at the thought of changes.

"It's about time." she said. "Grace never changed a thing in thirty years. It could do with a thorough gutting."

"Jimmy is giving me a quote. And Darcy is coming over with some design plans. Would you like to look over them with us?"

"I don't think so Taylor. This is your home now and it needs some TLC in the hands of the young. You and Darcy will come up with some great ideas, I know. Too bad you couldn't get Maggie to help. She's got a degree in interior designing I think from before she became a real estate agent."

"Well, that's out the window now. I couldn't stay in a room for any length of time with her without conjuring up that image of her in black leather." Even a fleeting picture now brought a smirk to her lips.

"Well, on that note, I'm off," said Edie. "I'll collect Jasper and go out the back way."

"And you will talk to Andrew tomorrow?"

"I will."

That afternoon, just after two o'clock, Taylor took Tristan for a walk. Something drew her past the church. Curiosity, she guessed. A glance at her watch told her the funeral for Jonah would be underway and while she hadn't wanted to attend, she wondered who would.

She couldn't very well parade back and forth in front of the entrance to see who came out but she timed it well. She was walking down the back lane that ran from the church to the main street when she could hear the organ music begin a dirge-like air.

As the doors swung open, the casket made its way borne by pallbearers, to the hearse, on its way to the graveyard for internment. Rev. Steven was next to the doorway where he waited for mourners to file out to the waiting limo.

Taylor took refuge behind a garden shed that jutted into the alley. She felt a little like Nancy Drew hiding under a staircase to watch jewel thieves. She stifled a giggle and then a querying squeak from Tristan who couldn't figure out why they had stopped. His silence would only give her a couple of minutes, she knew, but she wanted to see who would be the mourners for Jonah.

A wheelchair came first, pushed by an attendant from the care home. Jonah's father. Taylor couldn't see his face but the dejected body posture told her this was probably the one person who grieved for Jonah. There was a considerable wait before Anna appeared in the door. She stopped on the step until her father was settled in the limo and deliberately waved the mortuary attendant aside, heading for the parking lot.

Shortly afterwards the rest of the congregation filed out. It was a small group, consisting mainly of the hardcore number that attended every funeral in Badger Lake.

Tristan began to tug at his leash and she turned to go back down the alley, away from the church. As she turned she did a double-take. There, in the continuation of the alley across the street, taking up a post in the shadows much like her own, stood a familiar figure. Hank! What was he doing there? As though he sensed someone watching the watcher, he turned and disappeared from sight.

Chapter
Sixteen

Next morning Taylor set out in her car. She had an appointment at the service station for an oil change—not before time.

"Thanks for fitting me in," she said to Ken, the mechanic and owner. She had gone to school with his daughter." I should have brought it in weeks ago, but it doesn't get a lot of driving, so I keep forgetting. How's Amy doing?"

"Great," he beamed. "She's expecting her third any day now. Frances is down there all ready to be present for the big event."

He gave his hands a wipe with a cloth that had more grease on it than the hands it was wiping. "Do you want to wait around? I'll do it right away."

"No thanks. I have some errands to run and I'll come back. In an hour?" He nodded.

She couldn't explain the feeling of discontent that had suddenly fallen over her. Why? Could it be the news that Amy, a girl her own age was just about to deliver her third child? That was ridiculous. First of all, Taylor didn't want three children. She wasn't sure she wanted any. And secondly she was still young. Besides, she didn't need children or marriage at all if she chose. Then why the feeling of discontent? Her mind led her back to Andrew and she swore silently at him. Tonight for sure she was having it out with him. Either they were in a relationship or they weren't.

She might as well check the post office while she was

downtown and pick up her junk mail. Why did she even bother? She didn't feel like coffee at the Northland this morning. She just felt like getting her errands done and going home for a long soak in the tub. Or maybe an epic walk with Tristan to shake off this unpleasant and unfamiliar angst.

Déjà Vu at the post office. Taylor clambered up the steps to check her mail and there was Andrew, standing stock still, staring at an envelope. He didn't even see her come in.

She was just about to ask him if Edie had talked to him yet this morning when he jumped and made a motion to stuff the offending envelope in his pocket. He missed and as he made a second attempt it turned in her direction so that she clearly saw the return address. It was a logo—not any logo but the one she and Edie had discussed at length yesterday.

Why would Andrew have a letter from a lab? If it was work, wouldn't it come through the station? This had to be private. Was Andrew doing DNA tests for himself? She tried to think of what she knew about his parents. He had never mentioned adoption but maybe he was and had finally gone about searching for his real parents, just like Anna.

She realized with a start that she and Andrew had been staring at each other wordlessly for more than a second.

"Gotta run, Taylor. See you later."

Still the inscrutable Andrew. But why would it never come up in their conversations if Andrew were doing an ancestry search? She knew he was a private person, but they talked about everything—or so she thought until recently.

She never did get a chance to ask him about Edie.

Instead she stopped at the hardware store to get some batteries and pick out a new toaster. Her old one had gone up in a puff of smoke that morning.

She looked over her shoulder at the checkout desk and saw Kelly standing by the door, her arms laden with two large bags, each holding what looked to be pillows or duvets, something huge and squishy anyhow.

"Hi Kelly," she said as she headed for the exit. "Day off today?"

Kelly spoke without looking at her. "Sort of," she said.

"Are you on your way home?"

"Yes," said Kelly. "That would be best, I think."

"Your arms are full. Let me give you a ride. I'm just

about to pick up my car."

She herded an unprotesting Kelly across the street to the garage. Her car was already parked on the street. She deposited Kelly and the bags into the car and took a minute to pay her bill with Ken.

Kelly stared straight ahead and didn't seem inclined to small talk so Taylor obliged with silence. Kelly looked as though she were in some sort of shock. Taylor wondered if she should leave her alone, so when they pulled into Kelly's driveway she picked up one of the bags, handing the other to Kelly.

It was the first time she had ever been in Kelly's kitchen. A friendly person, especially behind the co-op cash register, but not a really sociable one. That had always been her impression. Had she always been that way, or had it developed after marrying Hank?

They both set down the bags. and Kelly called out towards the living room, "Kevin, Denny?" She climbed the stairs and repeated her call.

When she came back to the kitchen she looked more puzzled than frightened at the nonappearance of her sons.

Taylor knew she couldn't leave Kelly alone in her dazed state. She pulled a kitchen chair out from the table and said. "Sit. Shall I make us some tea?"

Without waiting for an answer she put the kettle on and then sat beside Kelly.

"Don't you normally work weekdays, Kelly? Did you leave work early today?"

Kelly looked at Taylor. It seemed to take a great effort for her to focus. Finally she said, "Hank came in. He began yelling at me and after he left, the manager told me to take the rest of the day off because I was upset."

"So you went shopping?" Taylor pointed to the bags.

"Yes, that's what Hank was cross about. I'd forgotten to buy new bedding for Davy and Mike when he told me to. So I thought if I picked it up now he'd be pleased."

Taylor bit her cheek to hold the words back. Is that how Kelly had been living? Walking on eggshells to placate Hank at every turn and suffering when she didn't?

"So aren't the twins at Day Care? Don't you drop them off with Stella when you work?"

"Yes," she said. "The older boys are with their grandparents for the summer, and the twins go to Stella's. But when I went there to pick them up, Stella said Hank had come and got them earlier. Why would he do that? He's supposed to be working."

"Did you phone him to find out?"

"He won't answer his cell. It goes to message."

The kettle began to whistle and Taylor poured the boiling water into the pot. She tried to think who she should call for help. Because obviously Kelly needed someone.

"Is there no one I can get hold of to come and stay with you?"

Kelly slowly shook her head. "I don't have anyone but the boys," she said as she began to cry. "And now he's taken them too."

"He won't have taken them away Kelly. He probably got time off and took them out for a treat. He won't harm them. He's their father after all." Too late she realized the danger in the words she'd spoken.

Kelly's sobs became vocal now and she struggled to get the words out.

Shaking her head vigorously she said, "He's not. The twins' father that is. He tested them to find out."

"Did you know all along he wasn't the father?"

She nodded. "I was pretty sure. But I was scared. When Jonah dumped me, Hank came along. He asked me to marry him right away and when I found out I was pregnant with one of those tester things, I thought if I married him then it would be so close no one would ever know. It's all my fault. Why did I ever marry him?"

Taylor thought it strange that all her regret was for marrying Hank rather than getting pregnant by Jonah. Of course Hank had probably inflicted more pain on her than Jonah.

"I don't imagine Hank took the news well."

"He went wild." She began to rub her legs and Taylor was sure she was reminding herself of a beating she had received. Maybe Andrew was the one to call. But domestic abuse cases could sometimes go strange. It might make things worse to have Hank picked up by police.

"Then afterwards," Kelly went on, "He got really quiet and that was scarier still. He said he was going to make me pay. And that's what he's doing now. He has the boys and he's going to take them away from me." She stood up so quickly the chair fell over. "I have to go. I have to find him and the boys. Maybe he'll think I suffered enough and he'll let me go back with them."

The back door opened and Taylor wasn't sure which one of them jumped the highest. Hank stood, glowering in the doorway. "Airing our dirty linen in public, are you Kelly?"

"No, No," she said, her voice rising to a screech. "I haven't said anything. She's leaving now. I didn't tell her anything."

"Don't lie," he said quietly. "I've been standing outside. I heard you."

"Where are the boys?"

"They're somewhere safe away from their slut of a mother," he said.

"Please Hank. Please take me to them."

Taylor began to stand up from her chair. She didn't know what to do but wanted out of this house and away from the hatred in Hank's eyes. She would call Andrew and he'd get here before Hank had time to really hurt Kelly.

"Sit!" barked Hank. She sat.

"I've lived in this town all my life," Hank said. "I'm not about to become a laughing-stock now."

"You're not a laughing stock," whimpered Kelly.

"I will be if they find out Jonah is the father of your bas-tards. And I got taken in by their whore of a mother." Kelly flinched.

"No one needs to know," said Taylor. "I won't tell any-one."

"Of course you will. You are Miss Nosy Parker in this town. Everyone will know. That fool Jonah thought he'd get me to pay to keep it quiet. Well, I found a better way to keep him quiet. Now I have to find a solution for you."

Oh no, thought Taylor. Trying to talk herself out of Hank's anger over who was father of the twins was one thing. Hearing him admit to murder was another. He wasn't going to let her walk out of this kitchen to tell on him.

"Your friend the cop has been snooping around, asking me all sorts of questions. You probably put him up to it."

"No," protested Taylor. She realized Andrew had discard-ed the list of blackmail victims long ago. The misdeeds were too petty. No one would kill over fifty dollars here or there.

For Hank it wasn't the blackmail at all. It was the fact that Jonah was the father of Kelly's boys. Andrew's questioning of Hank meant he was leaning in his direction. After he talked to Edie would he be on his way here for another chat with Hank? She hoped so.

Hank held out his hand to Taylor. "Keys," he said. At her uncomprehending look he snapped, "The keys to your car."

Taylor reached into her purse, slung on the back of the kitchen chair. Her cell was in her purse, in another compartment. She looked up at Hank and he was watching her carefully as she withdrew the keys. No chance to grab her phone. She obediently handed him the keys. She had to think. Could she just make a dash for it—to the living room and out the front door. One scream out there would bring people running. One scream now should do the same. Had Kelly yelled when she got those bruises? No one had come then, but maybe she had learned not to make a sound, that it only made things worse. Or maybe neighbours were used to noise and yells coming from a house with four boys.

Hank gave her no time to plan. He leaned around the outer door behind him. He stood in the doorway now, a rifle in his hand.

"Out," he said to them, gesturing with the gun. Taylor's heart sank. There would be no dash for the door now.

Kelly slouched past Hank and Taylor had no option but to follow. Her eyes scanned the back yard. Would anyone be watching? Where were all the busybodies in town when you wanted one? But then the trees around the perimeter of the yard would probably screen them from view.

Standing in the outer porch, Hank handed Kelly Taylor's keys. "Get her car," he said. "Bring it around back."

Kelly did as she was told and Taylor's Focus pulled up beside the porch.

"Stay there," he said to Kelly who was opening the car door. "You're going to drive. Miss Busybody here and I will sit in the back."

"Where are we going? What are you going to do? Hank, you can't hurt Taylor." She finally caught on to the horror that was her husband. "You killed Jonah!" she shouted.

"Shut up and do as you're told if you ever want to see those boys of yours again. I had no choice. He was going to tell everyone he was the twins' father."

"But he didn't know," said Kelly. "I wasn't even sure. How could he know?"

"He was smart enough to guess. That was his mistake."

"Where did you take the boys, Hank? You haven't hurt them, have you?"

"What do you think I am? Of course I haven't hurt them. They are somewhere safe. You'll see them if you do as you're told. Once this one is taken care of, we're going to leave Badger Lake. We'll move somewhere that's never heard of Jonah Whitcomb and start new. No one ever needs to know about this."

He directed Kelly out the north road of town and in the direction of the river valley.

"Your friend is going to have a terrible road accident," said Hank. "Unfortunate, but these things happen. Just last month someone went off the big slope at Cooper's Corner. She'll never pry into other people's business again."

"Hank, no!!" Kelly. She swung the car violently to the right as she turned to look into the back seat.

"Watch the road!"

Chapter
Seventeen

The car sideswiped the railing that ran along the raised highway. Kelly slammed on the brakes and it skidded to a stop just past the railing, at a spot where the treed slope disappeared into the ravine.

"You stupid bitch!" Hank yelled. "Get moving!" But the right fender had crumpled into the tire and the car would only limp along.

"It won't go," wailed Kelly.

"Shut up. I have to think." He scanned the road. It was empty except for a car ahead of them coming in their direction. "Pull the car to the shoulder here. Stop it. Crouch down. No one can see the fender damage from that side."

Taylor crouched. She managed to hold up one hand behind her in a gesture but had little hope anyone would see it through the window or even interpret it as a cry for help. They would more likely assume someone was making out in the back seat.

Hank opened the door on the far side. He slid out, the rifle in a firm grip in one hand. "Now you Kelly. Slide over and out the side door so no one sees you from the road." Lastly he pointed at Taylor. "Now you."

Taylor knew this was her last chance. Hank might have to forego his planned accident but he still had plans to make her disappear permanently.

He held the rifle at an awkward angle. It would take time to aim and fire. She began to slide across the seat and just as Hank expected her to exit, his arm reaching for her shoulder, she grabbed the door handle and slammed it shut as hard as she could.

Hank screamed in pain as the door jamb connected with his wrist, but it was the other arm that held the rifle. Taylor flung herself back across the seat and yanked open the roadside door. She could see a car coming behind them. Surely Hank couldn't shoot with a witness driving by.

As she tumbled out into the road, she could see the car, brakes screeching, pull to the side of the road behind her car.

Andrew!

She tried to yell at him that Hank had a gun. She had nearly forgotten about Kelly.

As Taylor shouted her warning to Andrew, Kelly brought down her two hands, held together as a weapon onto Hank's right arm. In total surprise, he dropped the rifle. That was all the time Andrew needed to take control of the situation. In minutes he had flung the rifle to the side, shoved Hank against the car and had him in handcuffs.

Taylor could hear a siren. In no time at all the other cruiser pulled behind Andrew's and Hank was being ushered into the back seat.

Kelly lunged at the vehicle. "Make him tell me where the boys are! He's kidnapped my sons!"

Taylor wrapped her arms around her friend. "Andrew will find out," she said. "Hank might want to kill me but he won't hurt the boys. He will just be hiding them. They'll be safe. Probably with his parents."

Andrew came back then and looked at Taylor's car. "I'll send the tow truck," he said. "Joe has Hank under control. I'll take you and Kelly with me."

He turned to Kelly and said," Don't worry about the boys. I have Miranda calling Hank's family to locate them. We'll hear any minute, even if Hank won't tell us where they are."

His phone went off then and he turned from them to answer. When he looked back he had a grin on his face. "The boys were out at the farm with Hank's cousin. He had no idea what was going on. Hank told him you were sick and he had to work. Could the boys stay over? They're on their way back now."

Kelly collapsed against Taylor's shoulder. "I'm so sorry,"

she said. "This is all my fault. I could never stand up to him. It was bad enough before he found out about Jonah..."

"It's all over now," said Taylor, consolingly, but she knew it wouldn't be. Kelly would have to face the town's reaction to Hank's arrest, suffer through a trial, and find a way to raise four boys, her twins and Hank's two oldest, all on her own. It was going to be a daunting task. But she also knew the people of Badger Lake. They would rally around her and help.

Chapter Eighteen

The ride back to town was a silent one. Taylor sat in the back with Kelly and Andrew had the front seat to himself.

She tried once to ask a question but Andrew shushed her with a "Not now, Taylor. We'll sort it all out later." She had to be content with that—that and the fact she, Kelly and the boys were all safe.

It was the next day before she could find out what happened. Even Edie when she called said to get some sleep and they'd talk it out tomorrow.

She had finished breakfast and was about to pour a second cup of coffee when Edie appeared on her doorstep. She held a plate of fragrant, fresh cinnamon buns. "I hope you still have room," she said.

"For these, always."

As soon as they were seated and Taylor had demolished the better part of a bun, she wiped her mouth and said to Edie.

"Your story first. You talked to Andrew yesterday morning?"

Edie nodded. "I told him all about the envelope I'd seen and what we thought it meant. He didn't seem surprised. I think he was already suspicious of Hank. Then when he left me, he headed out to look for you. And I'm sorry, but that's all I know. The rest is Andrew's tale."

Taylor told her how she had picked up Kelly, how Hank had surprised him, how he hid the boys to ensure Kelly's cooperation and related the events of the final capture. She still had a lot of questions.

"How did Andrew know where we'd headed? How did he know Hank was with me? That's what I'd like to know."

Edie looked over her shoulder out the kitchen window that overlooked the front yard and the road.

"I don't think you have long to wait," she said. "Andrew is pulling up."

Taylor leapt up to greet him at the door. As she watched the SUV turn into the drive, she saw he had a passenger. A black and white head with tongue lolling out sat in the right seat. Andrew grinned at her expression and opened the door for Monty who followed closely behind him.

"You did decide to take Monty! I'm so glad!" She ushered the collie into the kitchen where he and Tristan became acquainted. Then she shooed them into the back yard to play.

"And you," she said accusingly to Edie. "You never said a thing."

"Andrew said it was a surprise and I'm good at surprises."

"I hope one of those is for me," Andrew said, eyeing the two buns left on the plate.

Taylor held the plate above him, "Only if you promise to be totally forthcoming and tell us everything. Then you can have them both if you like."

"I promise, I promise." She set down the plate and he finished half a bun before he began. "Edie caught me just after I left the Post Office. When I'd talked to her, I went looking for you. Someone said you had your car in getting an oil change so I talked to Bill. He said when you picked up your car, Kelly was with you and had some big shopping bags. I went to Kelly and Hank's house looking for you but couldn't see your car. When I tried your phone, I could hear it ringing inside the house. The back door was open so I went in. Your purse was there, you weren't, Kelly wasn't, your car wasn't. So I assumed the worst—that Hank had somehow decided you were a danger to him or that Kelly was saying things to you she shouldn't."

"But how did you know where we were heading? It could just as easily been the south highway or any other side road."

"You are underestimating the observation powers of a

small town. Waters, next door, saw your car leave and thought it strange that Kelly was at the wheel, especially when he could see you and Hank both in the back. He already had called the station. He hated Hank, knew what was going on next door but felt powerless to stop since Kelly just shrugged it off. He kept a close eye on him at all times. Now he thought he better report it."

Andrew stopped to wet his throat with a large gulp of coffee. "I tried to imagine what Hank was going to do and thought he'd likely arrange an accident for you. The best place for that was Cooper's Hill. To be sure, I stopped at the edge of town and Mavis Strange was in her front yard. She remembered your car heading north a few minutes earlier. And the rest as they say, is history."

Taylor looked at him until he was forced to say, "What?"

"I'm waiting," she said.

He only raised his eyebrows higher.

"You haven't yelled at me yet for getting involved in your investigation."

"Nope. Actually I was thinking you had shown great restraint and had stayed out of it. You couldn't be blamed for giving Kelly a ride home."

Taylor relaxed.

"Of course, only you would end up being the confidante of at least four of my major suspects," he counted on his fingers, "Brenda, Anna, Maggie and of course Kelly."

"Hmm." he added. "You do realize those four main suspects were all women. They do say the female is deadlier than the male."

"But none of them was guilty," said Taylor. "Last time I looked, Hank was short on estrogen."

"Okay. Okay."

Edie made a motion to stand. "My curiosity is satisfied now. But I think you two have more to talk about, so I'm going to head home. I'll get my plate tomorrow."

Taylor waited till the door had closed. "We do have a lot to talk about," she said.

"I thought we'd covered everything."

"Your murder maybe, but not why you've been acting so strangely lately. And why you jumped every time I ran into you in the post office. And why you avoided being alone with me."

Andrew looked genuinely astonished. "I did all that?"

"Yes."

A duet of barking came from the back yard and Taylor jumped to the door. "Tristan, Monty, come." The dogs protested a moment but eventually made their way to the house. "Tristan has taken a dislike to one particular shepherd that gets walked down that lane. Every time he comes he barks and barks at him. Now he thinks he's got a sidekick to help, he's worse."

Dogs settled, she sat and waited for Andrew to go on.

"That letter," he began, and then stopped as though searching for the words.

"Okay, dive right in." he said. "A few years ago I had a short 'affair' I guess you'd call it with a girl who later left town. I never heard from her after she left until a couple of months ago. She called to say she had a three year old boy and he was mine."

"Oh," was all Taylor could think of to say. Then the shoe dropped. "That's the reason for the test. I thought you were checking your own parentage. I never thought for a moment..."

Andrew raised a hand to stop the flow of words.

"The reason I was so 'off', I guess, was I didn't know what would happen if he was my son. It would have changed everything."

Including me, thought Taylor, taking note of his wording, 'would have.' She decided to follow suit. "Would you have married her?"

"Good grief no!" said Andrew. "Neither one of us would have wanted that." Silently Taylor questioned that. Why would she contact him now otherwise? Probably she left for another relationship and it was over so back to square one. She shushed herself mentally for being so catty and perhaps a teensy bit jealous?

"But, if I was the father I intended to be a part of his life, and to contribute financially, and — well everything a father should do I suppose. Except marry his mother," he added quickly. "Anyhow, I got her to send a sample of his DNA and I sent mine. The end result is I'm not the father."

"Are you relieved or disappointed?"

"Relieved, of course." Then he reconsidered. "Maybe a tiny bit disappointed. I do want to be a father someday, but not in those circumstances. Anyhow," he leaned across the table to take her hand. "I was afraid how it might affect our relationship, so I didn't want to tell you until I knew."

"You didn't trust me." Taylor pulled back her hand.

"It wasn't that. I just figured there was no sense in your imagining things that might not happen. You do have a wild imagination, Taylor. I thought it best to wait until I knew for sure."

She grudgingly offered her hand back, but Andrew stood up and pulled her towards him. "Does this make any difference in our relationship, Taylor?"

She decided to show, not tell. When she drew back from their kiss, she said "I think I'm still a little disappointed that you didn't confide in me, but maybe I would have done the same thing."

Andrew laughed. "Not in a million years," he said. "When was the last time you ever kept a secret?"

She punched him hard in the shoulder.

"Ouch!" he said. "I guess I deserved that. But we're okay?"

"Only if you promise me you'll never do that again. That you'll talk to me instead."

"I don't think the situation is going to come up again, Taylor. How many exes do you think I have running around out there?"

Plenty, said Taylor, but only to herself. She leaned into another kiss with Andrew and felt a wet nose on her hand. She looked down to see Tristan on one side of them, Monty on the other, both looking at them with questioning faces.

"Oh great" said Andrew. "It looks as though our blended family is going to get along."

He led her into the living room and closed the glass kitchen door, leaving the inquisitive eyes on the other side.

That's one reno I might just bypass, thought Taylor. Doors sometimes have their uses.

About the Author

Sharon McGregor is a west coast transplant from the Canadian prairies, on a mission to escape the cold. Her imagination and story weaving got its start when she was an only child living on a farm. She's moved on from cowgirl dreams to romance and mystery, but hasn't lost her love for horses.

She writes humour, romance and cozies, sometimes a combination of all three. When not writing or reading, she is often found walking the dogs along the ocean. In spite of her attempts to escape winter, she loves watching her grandchildren at figure skating and hockey. The main item not yet ticked on her bucket list is travel. She wants to set her foot on six continents—she'll give Antarctica a pass, thank you.